M

Ferrars, E. X.
    Beware of the dog

M

Ferrars, E. X.
    Beware of the dog

Mynderse Library
31 Fall Street
Seneca Falls, NY 13148

BEWARE
OF THE
DOG

Books by E. X. Ferrars

BEWARE
OF THE
DOG

E. X. Ferrars

A Perfect Crime Book

DOUBLEDAY

New York   London   Toronto   Sydney   Auckland

A Perfect Crime Book

PUBLISHED BY DOUBLEDAY

a division of Bantam Doubleday Dell Publishing Group, Inc.
666 Fifth Avenue, New York, New York, 10103

DOUBLEDAY is a trademark of Doubleday, a division
of Bantam Doubleday Dell Publishing Group, Inc.

Library of Congress Cataloging-in-Publication Data
Ferrars, E. X.
Beware of the dog / by E. X. Ferrars.
p.   cm.
"A Perfect Crime book."
I. Title.
PR6003.R458B48   1993
823'.912—dc20   92-22134
CIP

M

ISBN 0-385-42288-1
Copyright © 1992 by M. D. Brown
ALL RIGHTS RESERVED
PRINTED IN THE UNITED STATES OF AMERICA
JANUARY 1993
FIRST EDITION IN THE UNITED STATES OF AMERICA

CHAPTER 1

As funerals go, Helen Lovelock's was a cheerful one. That was because she had been eighty-eight when she died and all her oldest and closest friends who would truly have grieved at the loss of her had died before she did. But a fairly large number of people came to the crematorium. She had been a figure of some note in the small town of Allingford. In her time she had been on a number of committees that had administered the town's affairs, she was rich and known for her charities, and she had kept to the end a collection of bridge-playing friends. My mother had been one of these, which was how I had been drawn into her circle when my marriage broke down and I had returned to live in Allingford in the house which my mother had left to me when she died.

While I still lived in London with my husband Felix I had let the house furnished, but when life with him had become something more than I could tolerate I had fortunately succeeded in getting rid of my tenants and had moved into the pleasant little house in Ellsworthy Street. I had also been lucky enough to get back my part-time job as a physiotherapist at a clinic in the town, and although I had never played bridge, Helen Lovelock for my mother's sake had often invited me to her home and I had become very fond of the independent, dignified old woman. So as a matter of course I went to her funeral.

Her death had been no surprise to anyone. For some years she had been troubled by her heart and one evening she had been found sitting serenely dead in a chair by her fireside. In the small crowd at the crematorium there were a number of faces that I knew, but I had no inclination to stay and talk to anyone till Anna Cox put her hand on my arm.

'You'll come back to the house and have a sandwich and a glass of wine, won't you?' she said. 'I'm asking only a few special people.'

Anna Cox was about seventy and she had been the house-keeper and friend of Mrs Lovelock for about thirty years. She was a short, stocky woman with grey hair which was still thick and which she wore cut short and brushed smoothly back from her rather heavy, square face. She had glinting grey eyes that needed glasses only for reading, a short nose, a wide, slightly down-curving mouth and a stubborn chin. For the funeral she was wearing a grey raincoat buttoned up to her neck although the early autumn day was fine, but in which I had seen her trotting about the town on the errands that she enjoyed ever since I had known her. That was now for about five years and it seemed to me that there had been no changes in her in all that time. That this impression was probably only the result of the changes in myself having kept pace with those in her was something that I realized, but all the same I was fairly sure that the wrinkles in her sallow skin were no deeper than when I had met her first and that she would look hardly older when she was eighty.

But what was she going to do now, I wondered, as I followed her out of the building into the cool October sunshine. I felt a little surprised at myself for not having thought about this before. Of all the people moving now towards their cars and setting off to their homes for lunch, she was the one whose grief must go the deepest and whose whole life was about to be altered by Helen Lovelock's death. How would she spend her time? Had she any relatives? Any friends? It was strange to realize how little I knew about her after having known her for as long as I had.

Mrs Lovelock's home had been a sprawling bungalow in

Morebury Close, a development on the edge of the town that had been built soon after the war. She had moved into it when the stairs in the Victorian mansion in which she and her banker husband had lived for most of their married life had become too much for her, and although she could easily have afforded to have a lift put into it, she had said that she would feel better in a bungalow. She had soon set about enlarging and modernizing the one that she bought and had made it charming and comfortable.

It was white, with a red pantile roof and a green front door, and was considerably more cheerful-looking and impressive than the other bungalows in the Close. It had nearly an acre of garden and twin garages, one for the car that she had once driven herself and one for Anna's. Nearly all her furniture was modern. She had spoken to me once about the mistake that many old people make of letting their surroundings become as old and worn as themselves, adding that of course she could not have kept the place as she liked it if it had not been for Anna. It was Anna who had seen that there were always fresh flowers in the vases, that the chair-covers and curtains were cleaned, that rooms were redecorated when they began to look a little shabby. It was to this bungalow that I drove after the service for my sandwich and my glass of wine.

It turned out that a sandwich and a glass of wine was more than a little of an understatement. There were sandwiches, it is true, made with pâté that I thought was certainly homemade, mixed up with lettuce and spring onions. There were small triangular objects made of the lightest of puff pastry filled with some kind of creamy seafood. There were biscuits spread with a variety of things and decorated with olives and small strips of green peppers. In fact, it looked to me as if Anna must have spent a good deal of her time between Mrs Lovelock's death and her funeral in preparing the baked meats for this occasion. Perhaps it had helped her to do it. She had done all the cooking in the household for as long as I had known her, with only the assistance of Mrs Redman, a woman who came in in the mornings to do the cleaning, to keep everything up to Mrs Lovelock's standard.

I had left my car in the drive among the few others that had arrived ahead of mine and on going up to the green front door I found it standing open, so I had no need to ring the bell as I went in. But my arrival was announced by the barking of Boz, the old Staffordshire bull terrier who had been Mrs Lovelock's special pet. There had been a time when she had bred bull terriers and sold them, but in the end this had become too much for her and she had let them all go except Boz, who had wound himself deeply into her affections.

He must be twelve or thirteen years old by now, I thought. The empty kennels of all the others were still at the end of the garden behind the house and were filled with garden tools, old sacks, watering-cans and the other odds and ends that accumulate over the years in any household. Boz sniffed at me carefully, allowed me to pat him and decided that it was safe to grant me admittance to the house before turning with his still raucous bark to greet people who were coming in behind me. I went into the drawing-room where Anna's party was being held and let a tall young man whom I had never met before put a glass of white wine into my hand.

I said, 'I believe you must be Nick Duffield.'

He smiled and said, 'That's me. And you are—?'

'Virginia Freer. My mother and Mrs Lovelock were friends for years.'

'Ah, I've heard of you.'

What I had heard of him was that he was a grand-nephew of Helen Lovelock's, only recently arrived from Australia to which he had been taken by his parents when he was only twelve or thirteen years old. He looked now as if he were in his early thirties and was strongly built, with broad shoulders, slim, long legs and big hands which at the moment were holding a tray of glasses. His face looked pleasant and friendly. His features were blunt, his mouth was wide, his eyes, under straight eyebrows, were a clear blue. His hair, of a light brown, was curly and cut short, showing that he had a well-shaped head. His skin still had the tan that had come from living for years in the Australian sunshine. His speech had a not very noticeable Australian twang.

'You haven't been here long, have you?' I asked.

'Only about three months,' he answered. 'Hardly time to get to know Aunt Helen.'

'But I know she was very anxious that you should come over before—well, before she died,' I said. 'Of course she knew that might happen soon. I believe you and Kate Galvin are her only relations. Is Kate here today?'

'My cousin—or is it second cousin?—I get confused about it,' he said. 'No, she isn't here, though I know Anna expected her. Now there's a wonderful woman, isn't she? Anna, I mean. I wonder how my aunt ever had the good fortune to find her. There are very few like her.'

At that moment I saw Anna beckoning to me from across the room, so I went on towards her, giving the people who had come in after me a chance to receive their glasses of wine. Anna had shed her grey raincoat but was still in grey, a plain neat jersey dress with just one ornament on it, a brooch of diamonds and pearls which I knew was valuable and which had been an unexpected gift to her from Mrs Lovelock, whose impulses of generosity were frequent but nearly always sudden and unpredictable. It had not been for Christmas or Anna's birthday or any special occasion that the brooch was given to her. She had shown it to me at the time with a shy sort of pride as if it somehow aston-

ished her to have earned the affection that the gift ex-
pressed. She was absently fingering it now as she thrust a
plate of sandwiches towards me.

'You haven't met Nick before, have you?' she said. 'He's
a dear boy. But it's so sad he didn't come over long ago.
Helen took to him immediately and it would have made
such a difference to her, these last few years, if she'd been
able to see him, even if it was only now and then. I know
he'd never have moved in here to live with her. He'd have
wanted a job and perhaps he wouldn't have been able to
find one in Allingford, or even if he could have, he might
not have wanted to stay in a dull little place like this. But
at least he could have come for the odd weekend. It's no
good regretting that now, though, is it?'

'But he's been staying with her ever since he came over,
hasn't he?' I asked.

'Yes,' she said.

'What about his parents? Are they both dead?'

I knew that his mother had been the daughter of a sister
of Mrs Lovelock's.

'Yes, and it's a sad story,' Anna said, 'because his father
drank himself to death out of sheer loneliness on a sheep-
station somewhere in the wilds and then his mother committed suicide. Nick was quite young when it happened,
but he got himself a job with a big firm of builders in Sydney
and he was so intelligent and so hard-working that he did
very well and became something quite senior in the firm
and quite easily got leave to come over when Helen wrote,
begging him to come so that she could get to know him. Of
course she offered to pay his expenses, but he said he didn't
need any help.'

'Is he gong back to Australia?'

'I expect so. We haven't talked much about it.'

'And Kate?' I said. 'Nick said you expected her.'

Kate Galvin was the granddaughter of another sister of

Helen Lovelock's. She was an actress and had been in Hollywood for the last three years, not spectacularly successful, but managing to make a name for herself in a small way. Like Nick Duffield, she was an orphan, though the end of her parents had been more commonplace than this. They had driven in their small car head-on into a collision with a lorry. Kate had been about eight at the time and Mrs Lovelock had taken over the expense of her education and given her a home for her holidays until the girl had gone to a dramatic school and then on to the stage. She must be about thirty now, I thought. I had met her a few times during her visits to Allingford, but I did not know her well.

'I did expect her, yes,' Anna said. 'I sent her a cable when Helen died and told her when the funeral was going to be. Not that I really thought she'd come, but only last night she telephoned that she'd be here in time for it. She telephoned all the way from New York and d'you know, her voice sounded as clear as if she was calling up from somewhere in Allingford? Wonderful, isn't it, what they can do nowadays? I suppose something on the journey's delayed her, or perhaps she changed her mind and decided not to come after all. Ah, there's Dr Cairns.'

She left me to talk to the young doctor who had attended on Mrs Lovelock for the last two or three years, after his predecessor had retired.

I turned to talk to the Hearns, who were standing near me. Roderick Hearn was a lecturer in economics at Allingford's Polytechnic and Margot, his wife, had surprised everyone recently by writing a detective story which had been unexpectedly successful, even finding its way on to television. They lived in one of the bungalows in Morebury Close. Roderick was about forty, a tall, thin, slightly stooping yet very handsome man, with a pale, narrow face with finely moulded features and big, intense dark eyes. It was an emotional and expressive face, though in fact he was shy and reserved. Margot was about ten years younger than her husband and was a tall, graceful woman with dark brown hair that she wore loose on her shoulders, an oval face, fair skin and eyes as dark as his, but which told you very little about her except that she was intelligent and observant.

Their relationship with Mrs Lovelock had been neighbourly rather than intimate. Neither of them played bridge, but from time to time she had invited them in for drinks, as I did myself, though they very seldom returned the invitation. They seemed to be deeply absorbed in each other and not in need of much contact with the world around them.

I said to them, 'Anna's just been telling me that she expected Kate Galvin today.'

Then as soon as I had said it I wished that I had not, for I had suddenly remembered that there had been a time when it had been said that Roderick Hearn had been engaged to marry Kate. For what reason nothing had come of it, whether it had been her doing or his, I did not know. I also did not know if it had left any scars and as a matter of fact I did not even know for certain that the rumour had been true.

They both responded with slightly satirical smiles.

'She'll come,' Margot said. 'She'll want to take charge of her affairs.'

'Not that she couldn't safely leave that to old Bairnsfather,' Roderick said. I knew that an elderly Mr Bairnsfather in London had been Mrs Lovelock's solicitor. 'But perhaps the presence of an unknown nephew on the spot has made her nervous.'

'You're talking of what they've inherited from Mrs Lovelock,' I said. 'Did she leave them much, do you know?'

'Everything, so Anna told us,' Margot replied. 'Half and

half between the two of them. Very nice for them, considering how little they've ever done for her.'

'Surely she can't have left them everything,' I said. 'She'll
have provided for Anna.'

'One would assume so,' Roderick said, 'though Anna
said nothing about it when she was talking about it all to
us. Perhaps she didn't feel it would be seemly to mention
her share.'

'Anyway, I suppose Kate and the nephew will have to
agree about whether or not to sell the house and so on,'
Margot said. 'It must be worth a good deal.'

'Has Anna said anything about what she means to do?'
I asked. 'I don't suppose she can stay on here.'

They both shook their heads.

'I shouldn't think she's had time to think about it,'
Roderick said. 'I should think a good old people's home
would be the best thing for her.'

'Only those places, the good ones, are terribly expensive,'
Margot said, 'so that'll depend on what Mrs Lovelock's
actually done for her. Of course she's too old to look for
another job.'

'I wouldn't mind giving her one myself, if I could afford
it,' I said. 'I think it would be heaven to be looked after by
Anna.'

'Ah, of course she's a wonderful cook and very vigorous
for her age,' Roderick said, 'but I can't see her settling
in now with anyone new. She could always manage Mrs
Lovelock and run things here just as she wanted.'

Something cold and moist had just been thrust into my
hand which a moment before had been holding a sandwich
but now was hanging loose at my side. I looked down and
saw the old bull terrier, Boz, appealing for a little attention.

'And I wonder what's going to happen to you, old boy,'
I said as I stroked his head. 'Anna won't be able to take
you with her into an old people's home.'

'He'll have to be put down,' Roderick said. 'He's so old, he must be near that anyway.'

'Put down,' Margot echoed him. 'That sounds so nice and merciful, doesn't it? All in his own interests. But I wonder why people can't just say they're going to have him killed.'

She gave a rather eerie little giggle that made me look at her, wondering, not for the first time, what kind of person she really was.

It was some time before I had another talk with Anna. In the meantime I had eaten one sandwich, two or three little triangles of puff pastry and had had my glass of wine topped up more than once by Nick Duffield. Then I had sat down on a sofa where Paul Kimber came and sat beside me.

Paul had been Mrs Lovelock's next-door neighbour for several years. He as a freelance journalist, writing articles mostly about gardening, wild life and other aspects of nature, and maintaining a garden full of luscious-looking fruit and vegetables. He spent a little of his time painting quite attractive watercolours and sometimes making jewellery which he sold in a craft shop in the town. I doubted if he ever had an idle moment, his life was so full of interests, but I assumed that he had some private income as it seemed unlikely that his journalism or his jewellery could maintain him in the comfortable way that he lived. Not that his bungalow was more than half the size of Mrs Lovelock's and I understood that he did all his own cooking and cleaning. He was about forty-five, unmarried, a short, square man with the beginnings of a paunch which was encased at the moment in a sagging pullover, over which he wore an ancient tweed jacket. He had a high, bald forehead and a fringe of dark hair, a small, dark beard and wide, grey, very innocent-looking eyes. I had never entirely believed in their innocence, for I had noticed that he could be quite spiteful when he chose, though to do him justice this was not often.

As he sat down beside me he asked me how I was and I replied that I was very much as usual, then he said, 'I was in London a few days ago, seeing an editor, and I happened to run into your husband. We had lunch together. He told me he'd just come back from Singapore where he'd had the best Chinese food he'd ever eaten. He said he was going to do some articles about it.'

I thought I caught a hint of that malicious gleam that I knew in his mild grey eyes and wondered how far, if at all, he had believed what Felix had told him. Felix, with whom I had managed to live for three years before deciding that the strain of it was really too much, though we had never actually bothered about a divorce, had some excellent qualities. He was good-natured, good-tempered, affectionate and generous, but he happened to be a fairly extreme case of the pathological liar. He lived in a world of fantasy that was quite foreign to me. It was just possible, I thought, that he had been writing articles recently on Chinese cooking, but if so he had certainly obtained his information about it from some Chinese cook with whom he had made friends and who worked in Soho. I was sure that he had never been to Singapore.

I did not believe that he had ever been abroad. During our marriage I had wanted to go to Italy and to Greece and a few other places, but he had insisted that he suffered from fearful claustrophobia in aeroplanes and was devastatingly sick on the sea. In fact, he never went any farther from London than he could help. If the Channel Tunnel is ever finished some woman with whom he is involved may be able to force him through it to Paris, but I expect he will have found out by then that tunnels are as claustrophobic as aeroplanes.

'He didn't know about Mrs Lovelock's death,' Paul

Kimber went on. 'He said if he had he'd have come to the funeral, but he just couldn't fit it in at such short notice. I didn't know he knew her.'

'He did, just slightly,' I said. 'There've been times when he's stayed down here now and then.'

'You've managed to stay friends then,' he said.

I had a horrid feeling that in another moment he would be saying that that was very civilized. When a husband and wife have ceased to take pleasure in each other's company, yet have no desire to gouge each other's eyes out, cut each other's throats or even spit at one another, people have a terrible way of calling it civilized. The dreadful chiché does not rate civilization very high. I decided to get off the subject as quickly as possible.

'Have you talked to Nick Duffield?'

'Oh yes, we've been seeing quite a bit of each other these last few weeks since he arrived,' he replied. 'He remembered the people who had my bungalow before me, a couple who went off to some job up North. He used to spend quite a lot of time here with his grand-aunt before his parents took him off to Australia, but I don't think he'll stay on now any longer than he must to get his affairs sorted out. He's a rich man now, of course, and Kate's rich too. I wonder what she'll do with it. I believe she'll drop the stage and perhaps buy a villa in Portugal, or something like that. He'll go back to his job, I think.'

'You don't think idleness would suit him?'

'Not for long, anyway. To be successfully idle, like me, you really need an awful lot of things to do.'

I thought of Felix, who had a wonderful talent for idleness. He could lie on a sofa, doing nothing but chain-smoke and dream for hours at a time in complete contentment.

'Have you been doing anything of special interest recently yourself, Paul?' I asked. 'Making any more of that pretty jewellery?'

'Why don't you come in sometime and see?' he said. 'As a matter of fact, I've just finished a rather nice set of malachite and silver—a brooch and some earrings. And I've done a very charming necklace of many-coloured agates. But of course I'm no professional. I only play at it. And at this time of year I've been mostly involved with the garden. I've had a wonderful crop of apples.' He looked down for a moment into his glass of wine and gave a sudden sigh. 'You think I waste my time, don't you, Virginia? You'd like me better if I dedicated myself seriously to something or other—say music, or science, or, heaven knows, even crime, if it was clever enough. I've sometimes thought about that, you know. It must be very engrossing.'

'But I like you as you are, Paul,' I said. 'Certainly much better than I would if you were even the subtlest of criminals.'

'But I'd be very surprised if you've ever felt any respect for me. I very much doubt if anyone has ever respected me.'

'What a strange thing for you to say. You're in rather a strange mood today, I think.'

'Doesn't death do that to one, even the death of a very venerable old woman with a bad heart, whom one's been expecting to die for years? It makes one try to add up what one's made so far of one's own time, and when I do that it seems to me that I haven't really much of a harvest. Now when young Duffield gets to my age you'll see he'll be able to look back and say that though he started almost nowhere, which he did, you know, he's really built up something in which he can take pride, whether it's economically, or technically, or just humanly.'

'How d'you know that?' I said. 'He may look back and say what a mess he's made of his life, compared with that nice man he used to know in Allingford who got so much pleasure out of just growing apples and making nice jewellery. But this really doesn't sound at all like you, Paul.'

'It doesn't, does it?' He gave me a quick smile which showed a row of fine teeth in the midst of his beard. 'I think I want another sandwich.'

He got up and left me.

I looked round the room for Anna, thinking that it was time I said goodbye and went home. But she was talking to a couple whom I did not know, so I stayed where I was and almost immediately Julia Bordman and her son Charlie came to join me.

She sat down on the sofa beside me and he stood in front of me, looking down at me with the vague, slightly vacant stare that was normal to him. Whenever one met Julia or Charlie they were always together. How they arranged things in their home I did not know. It was a sad thing, but Charlie was what is called mentally retarded and Julia was the most devoted of mothers. It had ruined her marriage. Her husband had left her because of her dedication to the child, who now was about thirty-eight and who had spent a number of those years in a mental hospital before it was thought that he was well enough to be returned to his mother's care.

He was very polite and was gentle and quiet and except for the way that he always stayed near to her when they were out together and the emptiness of his gaze, he might never have drawn attention to his disabilities. He could talk rationally and pleasantly. He was a tall, good-looking man with thick blond hair which was always very carefully cut, delicate features and pale blue eyes under fine arched eyebrows. He was always very neatly dressed and had an odd air of being a little vain about his own appearance. Julia was nearly sixty, an angular, bony woman with hair that had been fair like her son's but which was now turning grey, features that must once have been as charming as his but were becoming unattractively sharp, and blue eyes which perhaps in contrast to his always struck me as being peculiarly alert and penetrating. The Bordmans did not live in Morebury Close, but some distance away in a block of flats near the centre of the town.

'I'm glad that's over,' Julia said. 'We very nearly didn't come. I didn't know what Charlie'd make of it. I sometimes think he doesn't know the meaning of death.'

She always spoke of Charlie as if he were not there, although he was always at her elbow.

'I'm glad I came,' he said in his soft voice. 'I liked it. I always like going to things.'

'It's true, he does,' Julia said. 'He's really very sociable. I knew he'd like the funeral itself because of the music and the solemnity. He takes things like that very seriously, and of course he's always been very musical. When he was a child he used to pretend he was a conductor and think he was conducting the radio. We still go to all the concerts we can.'

'I like Beethoven very much,' he said.

'That seems to be good taste,' I observed.

'Oh, he's got very good taste,' Julia said. 'In other things too. He chooses all his own clothes, and look how well-dressed he always is. And when I was having some new curtains made for the sitting-room he insisted on choosing the material, and really they were most successful. He's got a wonderful colour-sense. But I honestly don't think he understands about death.'

'Who does?' I said.

'I mean, he's like a child, he thinks poor Mrs Lovelock's gone away and he won't see her again, but that she's *dead* . . .' She gave a slight shudder. 'Anyway, I thought I ought to come, but when Anna asked us here I thought we'd better just go home. But as I didn't see . . .' She paused, obviously stopping herself saying something that she had nearly said by accident but which she was anxious to leave unsaid. I had no idea what it was. 'And Anna seemed very anxious for us to come,' she went on, 'and I feel so sorry for her, left stranded as she is. I imagine she'll be able to stay on in the house for a time, won't she? I mean, even if Mr Duffield and Miss Galvin want to sell it, it'll be better for them to have someone living in it to show people round than to leave it standing empty. So at least she needn't make up her mind in a hurry.'

'Mrs Freer, may I get you another glass of wine?' Charlie chose that moment to inquire.

'No, thank you,' I said. 'I must be going home soon.'

'I think I would like another glass,' he said. 'I like it very much.'

'No, dear, I think you've had enough,' his mother said. 'We must be going too.'

'Already?' he said. 'But we've only just come.'

'I think we've been here an hour,' she said. 'And this isn't just an ordinary party, it's something a little special.'

Yet the noise in the room, although several people had left by now, was that of a very ordinary party, with everyone talking a little louder than was really necessary. As the good things that Anna had provided had been consumed and the wine had been drunk, the rather uneasy sense of solemnity with which it had started had faded and the volume of chatter had increased till it was at least normal for any social gathering of the size.

Julia stood up and slipped her arm through Charlie's.

'Yes, we must go,' she said. 'Come along, dear, and say goodbye to Anna.'

'But I don't want to go,' he said. 'I want another glass of wine and another of those lovely little things with lobster in them. They're very good. Why don't we ever have them at home?'

His eyes looked as bland as ever, but there was a new stubbornness in his soft voice and I realized with surprise, because I had never seen it before, that he might be capable of making a scene if he was thwarted.

I saw Julia debating with herself whether or not to risk it. Perhaps it was the wine that he had already drunk that had produced the unusual little spurt of aggression, and perhaps, thinking this herself, she decided that to provoke him after a funeral of all times would not be worth her while, for she led him away to the table where the remains of the food were still laid out and helped him to one of the lobster canapés, though she prevented him refilling his glass.

As they left me Anna crossed the room towards me and dropped down on the sofa at my side.

'I think it's gone very well, don't you?' she said. 'I think it's what she'd have liked herself.'

But her square face looked very tired and there were deep lines of strain about her mouth.

'I'm sure she would have,' I said, wondering how much sleep Anna had had during the last few nights. 'You must have been working very hard.'

'Well, Nick helped, you know,' she said. 'He did most of the shopping for me and he saw to the drinks. You haven't really talked to him yet, have you?'

'Not really.'

'We must arrange that sometime. You'll like him so much.'

'Perhaps you'd bring him over to see me one day soon.'

'May I do that? Yes, I'm sure he'd like it and so should I. I've felt completely shut up in this house all these past days. Not that I've wanted to go out, but now that the funeral's over I somehow feel different. People tell you you feel better once the funeral's over, however dreadful it is to go through. But you do think she'd have liked what I've done today, don't you?'

'Of course she would, Anna. You've done just right.'

'It's a pity Kate wasn't here,' she said. 'Which reminds me, I saw you talking to the Bordmans.'

Why Kate Galvin should remind her of the Bordmans, unless it was something to do with that rumour that I had heard, I did not know, but I agreed that it was a pity that Kate was absent.

'That poor woman, Julia,' Anna said. 'I was a little surprised to see her at the service. She and Helen weren't really the best of friends. But if she regretted it I didn't want to seem to remember anything, so I made a point of inviting her here, even though it meant having that pathetic boy as well. Not that he's a boy any more, of course, but it's how I always think of him. I can't think really why people like that aren't left in homes where people know how to look after them. Having him out cost her her husband.'

'In that case, perhaps he wasn't much loss,' I said.

'Oh, I don't know about that. There are things some people can't stand. I don't believe for a moment I could have stood looking after someone like Charlie for long. But I've been lucky, haven't I. Helen was herself right up to the end, or almost.'

'Almost? Almost to the end, or almost herself, do you mean?'

She gave a sad little smile. 'Both, I suppose. She did get forgetful. And she didn't even quite understand how the world was changing.'

I gave her a thoughtful look. 'What do you mean, Anna?'

'Nothing. Nothing special,' she said quickly.

'Have you had time to think what you're going to do now?' I asked. 'You'll be staying on here for a time, I expect.'

'Yes, Nick has already asked me to do that,' she answered. 'I'll stay until the place is sold. But of course that may not be long. It's what agents call a very desirable property, in such a nice, quiet district and yet so handy for town. And quite handy even for London. They haven't had anyone in yet to value it, so I don't know what they'll ask for it, but now I suppose they'll get on with that sort of thing. And when it's gone . . .' She stopped with a soft sigh.

'You'll be sorry to leave it,' I said.

'Oh yes.'

'Have you any family to go to?'

'No, I was an only child and if I have any cousins I don't know anything about them. I worked as a typist and looked after my mother, who was an invalid, until she died, then I came to Helen. That was in the other house, but we moved here quite soon after I came. That's thirty years ago now. I sometimes forget I've ever lived anywhere else.'

'But Mrs Lovelock provided for you, didn't she? You won't have to go on working, surely.'

She repeated her small, wintry smile.

'She thought she had, poor dear, but I told you she didn't understand how the world was changing. She meant to be generous, but one of the things she couldn't keep up with was the change in the value of money. She left me an annuity of five thousand pounds a year. She told me about it and said I mustn't worry, I'd never know want. But that was about twenty years ago and she never made a new will, so that's all I'll get. Oh, I shan't starve on it, but it won't go very far these days, will it?'

I could easily remember a time when five thousand a year would have seemed riches to me, as I supposed Anna herself had thought when Mrs Lovelock had told her what she was leaving her, and that that was how it had been intended. But there would be no luxurious old people's home for Anna, which was what I had been expecting.

'And it's an annuity,' she went on, 'so I can't even play around with the capital, starting up some little business of my own, or anything like that. Of course I've got savings, which will help out for a time.' She gave a brief laugh which

had a sardonic note in it. 'You know, if I'd wanted to, I
believe I could have stashed away thousands. The poor
dear left everything to me to settle and she'd never have
known it. And perhaps there are people who'll say I was a
fool not to do it while I had the chance. After all, I've
known all along about the five thousand, but I had an
absurd sort of feeling that she'd never die, or at least that
I'd die before she did. She seemed quite indestructible and
that meant I'd no reason to worry. I dare say I shan't
actually live for so very much longer, so I'll manage somehow for the time that's left.'

'Don't talk like that,' I said, though it struck me just then
that perhaps what she had said would turn out to be true
because caring for Helen Lovelock had been her reason for
living, and unless she could find some other reason perhaps
she too would quietly die. 'Do Nick and Kate know about
the annuity?'

'I don't think so. I don't know. He and I haven't been
talking about money yet—'

She was interrupted by sudden angry barking from Boz.

As he barked he moved stiffly towards the doorway, the
hairs on his back bristling. Someone had just come in at
the door. It was a young woman, slim, not very tall, with
a mane of tangled chestnut hair and carrying a small suitcase. I had not seen her for more than three years and had
never known her well, but I knew Kate Galvin at once.

Also, just for an instant, I saw two strange things. In the
dark eyes of Margot Hearn, turned towards the doorway,
I saw a sudden blaze that looked to me like hatred, and
on Kate Galvin's face, as she saw Charlie Bordman, an
expression of utter horror.

As I said, it was only for an instant and I could have
been mistaken.

CHAPTER 2

With her arm through Charlie's, Julia Bordman led him quickly out of the room, passing Kate Galvin as if she did not know her, which perhaps she did not. He gave Kate a bright glance of interest, but she had stopped to stroke Boz.

'Be quiet, you silly old thing,' she said.

Anna trotted rapidly across the room to her, threw her arms round Kate's neck and kissed her warmly.

'So you got here after all!' she exclaimed. 'But everything's nearly over.'

Almost everyone had left by then.

'I know, I'm so sorry,' Kate said. 'My taxi broke down on the way from Heathrow. I ought to have been here in lots of time.'

'Have you had any lunch? I expect you're terribly hungry and there isn't much left here, but I can get you something.'

'No, no, don't trouble. I'm not really hungry at all.'

Kate had put an arm round Anna's shoulders and her voice was affectionate. Since I had seen her last she had turned into a very beautiful young woman. She had always been attractive but she had been groomed and taught and had acquired a new poise which appeared to be quite unself-conscious, yet was really something, I felt sure, at which she had had to work.

Nick Duffield moved towards her.

'Are you my cousin Kate?' he asked.

'Yes, I'm Kate,' she said. 'And you're Nick.'

'Yes.'

They gazed thoughtfully at one another. Then she gave a quiet laugh.

'I shouldn't have known you,' she said.

'I believe I'd have known you anywhere,' he answered.

She shook her head. 'That can't be exactly true. How old were you when we last saw each other?'

'I should think I was about thirteen. It was twenty years ago that I was taken to Australia.'

'That means I was ten. They say twenty years do change a girl.'

'I remember the colour of your hair,' he said. 'I remember how I admired it.'

'I can't remember that you ever showed it.' She smiled. 'Perhaps boys of thirteen aren't very good at showing their admiration for little girls of ten. They're more inclined to think them just a nuisance.'

'Or perhaps the memory of little girls of ten isn't as good as it might be.'

He too had stooped to stroke Boz, who was continuing to take an interest in the newcomer as if he had a feeling that perhaps he knew her.

She said, 'You used to be afraid of dogs ever after that big fellow of Aunt Helen's flew at you.'

'To be honest with you, I'm still afraid under the surface,' he replied. 'There are things one doesn't grow out of, however rational one tries to become about them. I believe even old Boz could chase me out of the house if he gave his mind to it.'

'Boz would never do anything like that,' Anna proclaimed. 'He wouldn't hurt a fly. He wouldn't be much use if we had burglars, except that he might make a noise. Now, Kate, what will you have? Here's a sandwich left, and you'd like a glass of wine, wouldn't you?'

'Thank you.' Kate accepted them as Anna brought them to her. 'Anna, who were those people who left just now?'

'Do you mean Julia Bordman and her son Charlie?' Anna asked. She frowned a little as if the question disturbed her.

'Ah yes, of course, I remember. Julia Bordman and

Charlie.' It sounded as if the names had some special meaning for Kate, not too agreeable, but just then she caught
sight of Roderick Hearn and her expression changed completely. Her eyes, which were greenish and faintly shaded
with make-up, lit up with pleasure. 'Roderick!' she said.
'I'm so glad to see you. And Margot! Of course I ought to
have expected to see you here, or at least at the funeral, if
only I'd arrived in time. Not that I was really expecting to
see anyone here, except Anna and Nick, but I ought to have
known that Anna would organize something of this kind.'

For a moment I thought Roderick was going to step
forward and kiss her, but in fact it was Margot who did so.
Whatever the meaning of the look that I had seen for an
instant on her face, it had gone, leaving it a little blanker
than usual, but not hostile.

'Have you come back to England to stay?' she asked.

'For a time, anyway.' Kate turned again to Nick. 'Are
you going to stay here?' She was looking at him curiously,
as if in some way he had become more interesting than she
had expected.

'Probably not for very long,' he said, 'though I'm not
sure of anything at the moment.'

'Kate, you remember Virginia, don't you?' Anna said,
leading Kate towards me. 'I'm sure you met her the last
time you were here.'

'Yes, of course.' Kate gave me her smile. 'You've stuck
to Allingford.'

'Oh yes,' I said.

'I doubt if I'll do that, though I'd be glad if Anna can
put me up here for a little while. Can you do that, Anna?'

'Yes, of course,' Anna said.

'I don't want to be any trouble.'

'It'll be no trouble at all.'

'You're staying here yourself for the present, aren't you?'

'If you'll let me. You and Nick must decide about that.

The house is part of your aunt's estate, which she left
equally divided between the two of you. So I'm at your
mercy.'

Anna managed to make it sound almost like a joke, which
I thought was very creditable, considering that the truth
must be that she was very anxious about her future, based
as it would be on that five thousand a year.

'Has Nick been trying to turn you out?' Kate said. 'Is
that the sort of person he's become?'

It was obvious from the look that she gave him as she
said it that she did not think so for a minute.

However, he replied, 'Oh, I'd put her out in the street
this instant if I knew who'd cook my dinner tonight.'

'I expect you and I will have a good deal of talking
to do,' Kate said more seriously. 'Actually I don't know
anything about the will. Oughtn't a lawyer to be here to
read it to us? That's what always happens after funerals in
novels. And of course all the wrong people get the money
and it's very upsetting and dramatic.'

'Mr Bairnsfather didn't think it was necessary for him to
come,' Anna said. 'Actually we've none of us seen the will
itself, but he telephoned and told us what was in it. It's
quite simple. You and Nick were Helen's only relations and
she's left everything divided between you.'

'Except what she's left to you,' Kate said.

'Yes, of course,' Anna said. 'But everything apart from
that.'

'She did really take care of you?'

'Oh yes, don't worry about that now. We'll go into all
the details later.'

I saw Kate give Nick a very quick little glance and he
responded to it with the smallest shake of his head. Considering that they had only just met, there was a curious
air of complicity about it as if he was conveying some message to her, warning her not to press the matter further at

the moment. Presumably he knew about Anna's annuity, but did not think that it would be wise to talk about it just then.

Kate turned to Paul Kimber.

'And how are things with you, Paul?' she asked. 'You're still next door?'

'Yes, I think you'll find everything there just the same as it was when you were here last,' he answered, his teeth flashing again in his beard as he smiled. 'I've become a fixture.'

'And do you still mow Aunt Helen's grass for her? I always thought that was so noble of you.'

'Yes, I still do that. I like doing it, you know.'

'And you're still writing articles about the sort of birds and insects you find in your garden, and things like that?'

'Yes.'

'And making that charming jewellery?'

'Yes.'

'You make me feel as if I've hardly been away.'

It was Kate herself, I thought, who had changed more than any of the other people left in the room. Yet it was an indefinable change. I remembered that as a child she had been a wild little thing, given to rolling on the ground in mad games with Mrs Lovelock's bull terriers, and hanging upside down from the branches of trees and terrifying her grand-aunt that she would fall, then passing into a phase of being brilliantly athletic, so skilled at tennis that hints had even been dropped that she might become a professional. But once she had become stage-struck she had allowed nothing to interrupt her progress. In her early days, however, she had tended to go about in dirty jeans and men's shirts and to be interested only in fringe performances. The dignified young woman that she had become was only of very recent appearance. I wondered how deep it went under the surface. And what was the truth about her once having been engaged to Roderick Hearn?

Margot Hearn had just turned to Anna.

'We must be going, Anna,' she said. 'Thank you so much for everything you've done. I'm glad we came.'

'Oh, you can't go yet!' Kate exclaimed. 'We've only just met after all this time. You and Roderick must tell me what you've been doing.'

'Much the same as usual,' Margot replied.

'That isn't quite true,' Roderick said with a slight smirk. 'Margot had a novel published a little while ago and it's been very successful. Not that it's brought in much money yet, but it's had excellent reviews and we think it's going to be televised.'

'A novel?' Kate said. 'What kind of novel?'

'A detective story,' he answered.

Kate looked surprised and impressed.

'I love detective stories,' she said. 'Are you going to write lots more?'

'I don't suppose I'll ever write another,' Margot said with a certain sharpness.

'But why ever not?' Kate asked. 'Haven't you got a contract?'

'She's got a contract and she's begun a second book,' Roderick said, obviously not noticing that his wife, either from some kind of shyness or a desire to get away, did not want to talk about what she was doing.

However, Kate went on questioning her about it, as if she felt that to take an interest in Margot's activities was the right thing for her to do and Roderick listened and smiled. Anna tweaked me by the sleeve.

'They're going to like each other,' she murmured in my ear. 'I hoped they would. I'm so glad.'

I thought for a moment that she meant Kate and Margot, then I realized that she was talking about Kate and Nick.

'It would be so suitable, wouldn't it?' she said.

So she was already thinking that Kate and Nick might marry, though it startled me to hear the phrase used in this day and age.

'Isn't that going rather fast?' I said.

'Well, of course it is, but I can't help thinking about it,' she replied. 'Their ages are just about right, and they're both so good-looking, and you can see they've taken to each other.'

'Good-looking people have a way of marrying very plain people,' I said. 'It's said to be because they don't want competition.'

She shook her head. 'I don't believe that at all. I think it would be splendid. And then all Helen's money would come together again. And neither of them would have to be afraid that it was their money the other was after.'

'There's really enough for that, is there?' I said. 'I mean, however much people have, do they ever think it's enough? Look at the way people who've already got millions seem to feel they must work themselves to death to make millions and millions more, and sometimes they shut themselves away from the world and live just on toast and tea while they're doing it. People like Paul, who seem to know what's enough for them to be quite contented, are really rather rare.'

'So you think Paul's quite contented?' she said.

'Don't you?'

She hesitated, then said, 'I expect he is. I don't really know him so very well though we've lived next door to each other for so long. But of course Kate and Nick aren't inheriting millions, not enough to turn their heads. Helen was a millionairess, I believe, but now it'll be split half and half. And I suppose I'm just silly and sentimental. Kate will probably go back to America and Nick to Australia and they may never meet one another again.'

I thought that that was only too likely. People like Anna, I thought, had very little idea of what really attracted people to one another. I had never heard her speak as if there had ever been a man in her life. But from a look on Nick's face just then it seemed to me that he was ready to play at being attracted by Kate, even if this was relatively momentary.

'I've just thought of something,' he said, coming forward. 'Kate, you know Aunt Helen's emeralds, don't you?'

She broke off what she was saying to the Hearns and looked at him uncertainly.

'Her emeralds? I've heard of them,' she said. 'But I don't think she ever actually showed them to me. Not that I remember, anyway.'

'She'd some very fine jewellery,' Anna said. 'I don't know what you mean to do with all the other things in the house, but you ought to take a look at it before you make up your mind to sell it all.'

'I don't much care for jewellery,' Kate said.

The only jewellery that she was wearing was a thin gold chain round her neck. I found it difficult to imagine her in anything flamboyant. But perhaps this was only because she had dressed herself in what she had thought proper for a funeral. It might be that it was only her actress's sense of the rôle that she would be expected to play that had given her for today her air of quiet restraint.

'I don't remember Mrs Lovelock ever wearing much jewellery,' Margot Hearn said. 'She liked to wear shabby old things most of the time, as if she'd just come in from cleaning out the dogs, even after she'd got rid of them.'

'But she'd some beautiful bits and pieces,' Anna said. 'Mr Lovelock was always giving her presents of really valuable things. Some of them came from his own mother. But you're quite right, Margot, she didn't wear them. She used sometimes to wear some pearls he gave her, and her engagement ring, which was just a single diamond on a plain gold band. All the same, she always looked after all the things very carefully.'

'Where did she keep them?' Kate asked. 'In the bank?'

'No, I tried to persuade her to do that,' Anna said. 'I said having them here was a temptation to burglars, if word about them ever got about. After all, quite a lot of people knew what she had. But she said she sometimes liked to look them over, even if she didn't feel they suited her, or that they'd ever be right for the very few social events which were all she could cope with these last few years. And sometimes she liked to show them to people too.'

'She showed me the emeralds,' Nick said. 'Kate, you must see them.'

Paul Kimber was fidgeting. 'Yes, of course, sometime. But perhaps not just at the moment.'

I was puzzled by his tone and by the fact that he looked as if he intensely disliked the idea of showing them off just then. Perhaps, I thought, they were not the kind of thing that he liked himself, considering how different from them his own work probably was. That was assuming that he was one of the people to whom Mrs Lovelock had shown them. But almost certainly he was, knowing as she would have of his interest in jewellery, and they might actually have roused envy in him, if the workmanship was fine. But if they were merely a collection of highly precious but gaudy gems he might have found them meaningless.

'You don't mean she kept them in her room, do you?' Kate said. 'That really would have been asking for trouble.'

'No, they're in the safe in here,' Nick said. He crossed to a picture on the wall between two windows and lifted it down. On the wall behind it was what was obviously the door of a small safe. I had vaguely known that Mrs Lovelock had a safe somewhere, but not where it was.

'Who can open it?' Kate asked. 'Anna, can you?'

'As a matter of fact, I can,' Paul said. 'Only a few months ago she wanted me to do a job for her on those emeralds. The clasp was broken. I think it had been broken for years but she suddenly got the idea she'd like to have it mended, so she asked me if I could do it for her. Of course that wasn't my sort of thing at all, but I wanted to oblige her, so I took the necklace to a jeweller who's more in that line, and so that I could get it out of the safe she told me the combination. She couldn't reach up to it herself any more, but she told me what to do and later I put the case with the emeralds in it back for her.'

'She did more or less the same with me,' Nick said. 'She told me how to open the safe and what she wanted me to take out of it, then we spent an hour or so going over her treasures. I think she enjoyed it, even if she never wore the things.'

'Well, open it now and let me look at them,' Kate said.

Nick reached for the dial on the safe and began to twirl it.

At first I thought that it was not going to work, that he had not remembered the combination correctly, but then the door swung slowly open and I saw that there were piles of papers inside, tied up in bundles. They looked like letters and were perhaps from her husband and might go back through her long lifetime to her girlhood. There were also a few leather cases of the kind that contain jewellery. Nick reached inside and brought out one that was a little larger than the others. He clicked it open and put it down on the table in front of Kate.

There were the emeralds, set in an elaborate collar of gold. They were Victorian, I supposed, though I knew very little about such things, and it was easy to understand why Mrs Lovelock had never worn them. To set them off would have needed a long, slender neck, beautiful bare shoulders and a dress of some grandeur. Even then they would have been a little too splendid for most people. Probably they had come to Mrs Lovelock from her husband's mother, or even his grandmother. I could not imagine Helen Lovelock ever wearing them, even when she had been young and as I was sure, lovely, for she had kept a kind of beauty, even in her old age.

'Well, I really must be going, Anna,' Paul said, all at once in a hurry. Again it was as if something about the emeralds upset him. It was a little strange. 'Let me know if there's anything I can do for you, won't you? Remember, I'm always next door.'

He let himself out of the door, giving Boz a pat on the head as he went.

Nick suddenly picked the emeralds out of their case and clipped them quickly round Kate's neck. Against the black that she was wearing they glowed with a fiery green brilliance.

'Look at that,' he said. 'Don't you want to keep them?'

His hands lingered on her shoulders as he said it.

She seemed to flinch at his touch, took one look at herself in the mirror over the fireplace, then fumbled frantically with the clasp and undid it. The emeralds slid to the floor. She left them there until Nick had picked them up. There was some intense emotion on her face. It might almost have been a kind of hatred, or it might have been fear, but whether or not it was really either of them I did not know.

Later, when I reached home, I wondered why thoughts of hatred and fear had been so much on my mind that day. But it seemed to me that I had seen one or other of them for an instant on the faces of several people. For instance, on Margot Hearn's when she had first seen Kate. And it was possible, I supposed, that Margot felt a certain amount of fear of Kate if it was true that her husband had once been in love with her. And Paul Kimber seemed to feel a mysterious fear of the emeralds, which was very puzzling. And that look of Kate's that had worried me could possibly have been because she had suddenly caught herself lusting after the emeralds. That was probably something for which she was quite unprepared and which, in the circumstances, at her grand-aunt's funeral, with the solemnity of death in the air, had disgusted her. All the same, I did not understand.

Of course, death by itself always generates some degree of fear. It is at the back of our minds all our lives and we deal with it in different ways, sometimes by religions, sometimes by pretending that it is not going to happen, sometimes even by rushing to grasp it before its time, as if to get it over like a dose of bad medicine. Anna's party had seemed cheerful enough, but the cheerfulness could only have been very superficial.

A time came when I could look back on this mood of mine that stayed with me for most of the rest of the day and could have said that it had been simply premonition. But I am not much inclined to believe in premonitions, my own least of all.

When I had let myself into the house I made myself tea and carried it into the sitting-room where I sat down in one of the easy chairs and did my best to relax. The room was full of sunshine and was very warm. I had turned the heating on a few days before when the weather had suddenly become chilling, and even though it was not necessary today I had not troubled to turn it off. Anyway, autumn was coming and it might be cold tomorrow. There were some coppery leaves scattered over the small square of lawn that I could see from the window and the trees at the end of the garden were beginning to turn brown. I felt suddenly very tired and had one of my rare impulses to telephone Felix.

These came to me occasionally and I almost never gave in to them. For what had I ever had to say to him? He might have something to say to me, but if it was something too outrageous about himself, as it was likely to be, it would only have irritated me. So I drank my tea and presently slipped into a doze from which I awoke to switch on the six o'clock news. It was all as usual, bombs, floods, revolutions, politicians snarling at one another about somebody's statistics and share prices shooting up, or perhaps it was down, I forget which. I suspect it is a bad habit to watch the news too often, for it leaves one with the feeling that human beings honestly cannot endure peace. It holds some terrible threat for them.

Next day I had several appointments at the clinic and set off for it soon after breakfast. It was half past twelve before I started for home again, walking because the day was as fine as the day before and because I wanted to do some shopping on the way. I had just left the square in the centre of the town and turned into the street where the supermarket was when I met Nick Duffield. He had just come out of the supermarket and was carrying a plastic bag full of purchases. We smiled at one another and both hesitated for a moment, neither of us sure whether anything more would be expected of us, then he suggested that we might go into the Rose and Crown for a drink, and I turned back with him into the square towards the old inn which is much the best restaurant in Allingford.

It has a Georgian façade overlooking the square, but once you are inside you are among dark old beams supporting low ceilings and uneven floors with treacherous little steps here and there. A good many of the beams are genuine, though their number has been added to for the sake of picturesqueness and there is very modern concealed lighting among them. Nick and I went into the bar and he bought a sherry for which I asked and a half-pint of bitter for himself. I thought that he was looking tired and abstracted and wondered why he had troubled to invite me for this drink.

'I've been doing some shopping for Anna,' he had said as he deposited the carrier bag on the cushioned bench on which we had been about to sit down. But when he had brought the drinks and was sitting down beside me, he only looked a little blankly before him and seemed to have nothing to say.

Anna had said that he was good-looking and that that would match excellently with Kate's good looks, but I was not sure that this could really be said of him with his blunt features and his wide mouth, even though the blue of his eyes was attractive and I liked his curly brown hair and the tan that still survived from Australia. I also admired the hand with which he grasped his beer mug. It was well-shaped and looked large and strong and dependable. One of the reasons I miss having a man about the house is that there is no one with hands strong enough to screw the tops off the more stubborn sort of jar. I have to rely on a complicated gadget which sometimes does not work. Nick Duffield's hands, I thought, could cope with anything.

'Have you decided how long you're staying in Allingford?' I asked to try to get some conversation going.

'No, I kind of thought while I'm over here I ought to look around,' he said. 'I might even go to France and Germany and some of those European places. After all, I don't know when I may get another chance to do it.'

'But you're financially independent now, aren't you?' I said. 'You could do it as often as you liked.'

'Well, yes,' he agreed. 'I suppose so. Funny thing, though, the idea takes some getting used to.'

'You aren't married, I believe,' I said.

He smiled a little and shook his head. 'No.'

'But perhaps likely to be?' That might explain his air of uncertainty.

Again he shook his head and smiled again. 'I don't believe so.' Then he asked abruptly, 'What's this thing between Kate and Margot Hearn?'

'Is there something?' I asked, deciding not to tell him about those rumours concerning Kate and Roderick. After all, I knew very little about the matter.

'They hate each other's guts, if I'm to believe Anna,' he said.

'She'd probably know,' I said.

'Is she the sort of person you'd believe?'

'Anna? Oh, I think so. Why?'

'I just wondered. It's just that we had an idea of asking the people fairly close to Aunt Helen if they'd care to come in and choose some memento of her before the valuers get to work for probate and all that. That way there wouldn't be any tax to pay on the things, even if it isn't strictly legal. And when I said to Anna we'd ask the Hearns—I was thinking, you see, of the people who came to the house after the funeral—she said I'd better ask Kate what she thought of that before I started any telephoning, because Kate would probably say she didn't want Mrs Hearn in the place. And the same with the Bordmans. Anna said don't ask them, Kate won't like it. Then she changed her mind and said go ahead, I mustn't listen to her because she was just a silly old woman.' He paused, drinking a little of his beer. 'Kate doesn't like me, if it comes to that.'

'Kate?'

'That's right.'

'What's made you think so?'

'Just a feeling I've got. D'you know her well?'

So this was why he had invited me for the drink, I thought. He wanted to talk about Kate.

'Not really,' I said. 'She's been coming to Allingford at

odd times, and I've met her now and then, but I've never got at all intimate with her. She came much more often as a child than during the last few years. Mrs Lovelock was very fond of her.'

'I've been wondering if she's jealous of me,' he said. 'I mean, if she took for granted she was the favourite and thought Aunt Helen had probably forgotten my existence, d'you think that finding the money was equally divided between us might have made her resent me?'

'It's possible, I suppose. But I've a feeling you're probably leaping to conclusions about her rather quickly. If she's a bit reserved in her manner, it's only natural. A funeral isn't just the best of times to make warm new friendships.'

'That's true. I remember when my mother died . . . But you don't know about that.'

'I think I do know a little about it. Anna told me she committed suicide.'

He nodded, looking away from me towards a shadowy corner of the dark-beamed old room.

'Yes, took an overdose. Said good-night to me as usual one evening and the next morning she was dead. Left me just a short letter behind, saying she was sorry she couldn't face life any more. I think it was more than a year before I began to feel fairly normal again. I don't suppose it showed, but it was there inside me all the time.'

'How old were you when it happened?'

'Oh, it was quite a long time ago. I was only about twenty.'

'And you lived somewhere in the wilds in those days?'

'Yes, outback up towards Darwin, in the Northern Territory. My father'd made a mess of everything and drank himself to death. It was that that killed my mother.'

His voice had grown harsh as he spoke with the roughness of a deeply felt anger. Because he had turned his face

away from me and I could only see his profile I could still
see how he had thrust out his chin and how taut his lips
had become. So in spite of his general air of friendliness
and good-nature, I thought, he could be violent if he was
moved to it. Or could that possibly be a kind of charade, I
suddenly wondered, I was not sure why. Had his anger and
his grief really lasted at that intensity for all those years, or
was this expression on his face, which was almost a grimace,
perhaps not very much more than a habit?

'So then you moved to Sydney?' I said.

'That's right, and did quite well for myself.' He was
looking at me again, giving me his pleasant smile. 'Sheep
weren't my line. Not that they were my parents' either.
They'd have done much better staying in England, with
my father getting some safe sort of job in an office from
nine to five and no romantic ideas about getting back to
the great outdoors and all that. When he died I tried to get
my mother to come back here. I thought it'd be best for
her. But she didn't want to let on what a failure the whole
thing had been, so she took that overdose instead. And I
sold up the place and moved to Sydney and got the kind of
job I could do. I wrote and told Aunt Helen the whole
story, as she was the only relative I knew of in England,
and she used to write to me occasionally and sometimes
send me very generous presents. I'm glad I got here in time
to get to know her before she died.'

'Didn't you know you had a cousin, Kate?'

'Well, yes, saying I didn't was a mistake, I did, but I
always thought of her as a kid. That's what she'd been
when I last saw her and somehow that's how I went on
thinking of her, which was bloody stupid. All the same,
when she walked in yesterday, not even so very young
any more—what is she? Getting on for thirty?—it fairly
took my breath away. I hope I'm wrong about my
feeling that she doesn't like me. As you said, I may be leap-

ing to conclusions too quickly. We'll both be staying on in
the house for a time, so we may get to know each other
better.'

'Anna will be staying too, I suppose,' I said.

'Till it's sold, I should think, though she won't say what
she's meaning to do,' he answered. 'I'm going up to London
to talk to old Bairnsfather about what we ought to do about
the sale and all that. I know things like wills take an ever-
lasting time to sort out, even when they're quite simple, but
I'd like to make sure Anna's getting what's coming to her
right away. But that reminds me, I told you we're asking
a few people if they'd like to come up to the house and
choose some sort of memento of Aunt Helen. You'll come,
won't you? Wouldn't you like some odd thing to remember
her by?'

I was not really much attracted by the idea. Perhaps
it would have been different if she and I had been more
intimate than we were. But I felt that I could not
refuse.

'That's very thoughtful of you,' I said. 'Thank you.'

'Can you make it late tomorrow afternoon, say around
six o'clock or thereabouts? I'm driving up to London in
the evening to see Bairnsfather next morning, but I don't
suppose I'll be leaving till eight o'clock, or later. Anyway,
Kate and Anna will be there and they'll be expecting you.'

'Thank you,' I said again.

Soon after that we finished our drinks and parted and
I went into the supermarket and did my shopping there.
Walking home, I wished that I had not committed myself
to going back to the bungalow in Morebury Close the following day, but that could not be helped now. Which of
Mrs Lovelock's possessions would it be appropriate for me
to choose for myself, I wondered. It should be something,
if possible, for which I felt some genuine liking, but of course
not valuable.

For a moment I wondered if I should say that I would like to have Boz. It would save his life. But I was fairly sure that I should not do it.

CHAPTER 3

When it came to the point it was quite easy for me to choose something by which to remember Mrs Lovelock. It was a photograph in a plain black frame of Mrs Lovelock herself, surrounded by half a dozen bull terrier puppies. She looked about seventy in the photograph and when I picked it off the top of a bookcase in the drawing-room and asked if I could have it, Anna was delighted.

'I'm so glad you want that,' she said. 'It's just the kind of thing one doesn't know what to do with. One hates to throw it away, but of course it's got no value and unless there's a home for it to go to, if you know what I mean, it's bound to end up getting thrown out somehow. And I've got all my own photographs of Helen and they'll go with me when I leave.

'Then have you decided when you're leaving?' I asked.

She seemed to be in a very cheerful mood that day, smiling and hurrying about the room, making sure that her visitors had drinks. She was in dark grey trousers and a bright green turtle-necked sweater in which I had often seen her before and her wearing it signified that this evening was an entirely informal occasion. In the photograph Mrs Lovelock was dressed in the same way, though the sweater was black and even at seventy she had had a slender elegance very different from Anna's stocky sturdiness.

When I had arrived at the bungalow the front door had been open, as it had been after the funeral and the only visitor to be there already was Julia Bordman. For once Charlie was not with her. I wondered what she had done with him. Had she left him locked in his bedroom, or even tied to a chair somewhere in their flat? Was that what had to be done with him when he was left alone? But of course thoughts like that were ridiculous. It was probably he who clung to her and not she who insisted that he must always accompany her, and although it might have taken a little persuasion to get him to permit her to go out without him, no doubt she had managed to settle him down happily in front of the television while she took a little time off.

Anna did not answer my question because as I asked it Paul Kimber came in and she left me to go and greet him. Both Nick and Kate were in the room, Kate lounging on a sofa with a glass of what looked like gin and tonic in her hand and wearing dark trousers and an exotic-looking jacket of many colours. Her chestnut hair was in a carefully arranged tangle and she had long brassy earrings hanging from her ears. She looked very different from the restrained young woman in black who had appeared on the day of the funeral. Nick was standing in front of the safe, which was open, and was reaching inside it for something, I immediately supposed for the case with the emeralds in it, but what he brought out was a small packet of letters.

He turned to me.

'Look,' he said, 'the letters I wrote to her from Sydney. She actually kept them. She told me she had. They're a rather miserable little bunch, aren't they? I mean, I didn't take much trouble to please her. I guess I'll burn them.'

There was a fire alight in the fireplace and before I had time to realize that he meant what he said, he had torn the packet apart and tossed the letters into the flames. They rose up, flickering, the little bundle of papers consumed in a moment. The fire was hardly necessary, for the room was very warm, yet without it I believe it would have had an air of desolation, already a place in which nobody lived.

'What made you do that?' I asked.

'It's what I do with most old letters,' he said. 'I never keep them. I hate the thought of them getting into someone else's hands and having them pawing through all one's secrets, however harmless they are.'

'It's my impression,' Kate remarked, 'that Nick has more secrets than you might suppose. And not necessarily so harmless.'

'Haven't we all?' I said. I remembered Nick saying that Kate did not like him and thought that possibly he had been right.

'Not me,' she said. 'My life's an open book, unlike some. I'll tell you anything about myself you want to know.'

'Exhibitionist,' Nick muttered, making me think that perhaps by now her dislike was returned.

Paul Kimber, coming forward, said, 'I don't believe you for a moment, Kate. Anyone with your attributes who claimed to have no secrets is almost certainly a liar.'

'And what about you?' she asked. 'Have you so many secrets, Paul?'

'I've got my fair share of them,' he answered. 'Now I believe I'm to choose something to remind me of dear Helen.'

'Go ahead,' Nick said. 'Look around. Take your time.'

He closed the safe and turned to stand with his back to it, his hands in his pockets. He had sounded as if he were irritated and perhaps had begun to find something distasteful in what was going forward in the room just then. I wondered whose idea it had been that we should be invited there to help ourselves out of Mrs Lovelock's possessions, if it had been his or Anna's.

She was pouring out whisky for Paul.

'I know what you'd like to take away, Paul,' she said. 'That pair of Staffordshire dogs. You've always admired them.'

There was a pair of them on the mantelpiece, looking as blankly expressionless as they usually do. There were a number of other china dogs there of varying quality. Some looked as if they might have been picked up in a seaside souvenir shop, with crests on their sides. One or two had a good deal of charm. Mrs Lovelock had made a habit of collecting them. If one ever had occasion to take her a present it was quite safe to take her a china dog.

'Oh, those are just what I—' Julia Bordman began, then stopped abruptly, flushing a little, as if she felt that she had nearly made a serious social blunder.

'They're what you'd like?' Paul said. 'Then take them, take them.'

'But if you want them—'

'Not at all, not at all.'

'It's just that Charlie's always loved them—'

'Thank God somebody does,' Kate said, 'even if it's only Charlie.'

Julia gave her a long look in which there was something probing, as if she wanted to find out something about Kate, and Kate met it with a trace of mockery in her greenish eyes. I remembered that when she had first come into the room, too late for the funeral, she had suddenly seen Charlie and the expression on her face had been one of inexplicable horror. Then Julia had hurried him out of the room.

'I don't think I want them after all,' she said. 'For all I know, they may be quite valuable. They're antiques, aren't they? I don't want to take anything valuable. I think what I'd like is this.' She picked up a round glass paperweight of a kind that I believe comes from somewhere in Scotland. It had what looked like a moonscape inside it. 'May I have this, Anna, or would anyone else like it?'

No one else seemed inclined to put in a claim for it.

Julia put the paperweight into the large handbag that she was carrying and pecked Anna on the cheek.

'So sweet of you to think of this,' she said. 'I feel so glad to have something of dear Mrs Lovelock's.'

'Oh, it was Nick who thought of it,' Anna said. 'He's so

thoughtful—so *very* thoughtful.' Her heavy features lit up as she said it, as if she meant something special. He looked embarrassed and Kate gave a soft laugh, the sound of which brought a sudden scowl to his face. Something was going on between the three of them, I felt, that I did not understand. I was thinking that I would leave as soon as I could when Roderick and Margot Hearn came into the room.

Boz, who had been lying asleep by the fire, scrambled to his feet and started furious barking, then appeared all at once to be overcome by confusion at having barked so fiercely at people whom he recognized as friends and, stretching himself out on the hearthrug again, seemed to go back to sleep.

Anna was giving the Hearns drinks and telling them to look round and choose something for themselves that would remind them of their old friend. She told them that perhaps they would find something that appealed to them in the dining-room rather than in this room, almost as if she did not want them to linger in the room with Kate. Afterwards, when I looked back on that evening, I began to see all kinds of possible meanings in the things that happened, though at the time I only felt that in spite of Anna's efforts to make the occasion pleasant for everyone, Nick's idea, if it had really been his, which I somehow doubted, had not been a good one.

Julia said a hurried goodbye to Kate and Nick and followed Anna out of the room. I heard her saying goodbye to her in the hall. Then after two or three minutes Anna returned to the drawing-room, leaving the Hearns in the dining-room. Dropping into a chair, she looked up at me. I had just finished my sherry and was getting ready to leave.

'You aren't going yet?' she said. 'Come and sit down and talk to me.' She patted a chair near her. 'Such extraordinary things have been happening and my head's in a whirl. You asked me if I'd decided when I was leaving, didn't you?'

I remembered that I had. Sitting down beside her, I said, 'Well, have you?'

'Not exactly,' she answered, 'but Nick's going off to London this evening and he's going to see Mr Bairnsfather tomorrow and that may help to get things sorted out. For the present I just don't know where I am.'

'Is there something peculiar about the will?' I asked, wondering suddenly if it had turned out that there was more for Anna than her five thousand a year.

'Not about the will, no,' she said. 'But it's Nick, you see. He's offered . . .'

But she paused there as Margot and Roderick came back into the room. They had not taken long to choose their memento of Mrs Lovelock. It was a book, a copy of Wilkie Collins' *Woman in White*. A book was a very tactful choice, I thought.

'Margot would love to take this,' Roderick said. 'She's been saying that considering what she's trying to write herself, she ought to read up on her Wilkie Collins, and this has Mrs Lovelock's name written in it.'

'I'm sure she'd love you to have that,' Anna said. 'Of course, she loved Margot's book. She said she was sure she'd end up very successful.'

'And that'll be very nice for Roderick,' Kate said in a soft drawl, 'with cheque after cheque dropping in through the letter-box. Perhaps after all you won't have to spend the rest of your life in Allingford, Roderick. Perhaps you'll be able to retire to some exotic place and write something very important and profound about economics.'

I knew that she was referring to something in her own relationship with him, though I knew too little about it to sort out what it was. His only response was to look a little more expressionless than usual. But Margot looked as if she was finding it difficult not to lose her temper.

'We've nothing against Allingford,' she said. 'It suits us. And if Roderick were to hope he might some day live on my earnings, he'd only end up starving. He knows that only too well.'

'And he always was an impatient man, wasn't he?' Kate said. 'Always in a hurry to get nowhere in particular, or so I remember it used to seem to me.'

Roderick suddenly began to laugh. 'Very good,' he said. 'Very good. You've hit me off exactly. But it's the hurrying that's the great thing, isn't it? Does it matter where one gets to? Now, my dear, we'd better be going.' He put an arm round Margot's shoulders and steered her towards the door.

Anna jumped up from her chair and went with them to show them out. After a moment she returned and sat down again beside me.

'I was saying . . . ?' she said, as if she had forgotten what it was and wanted me to remind her.

'You said something about Nick offering you something,' I said.

She glanced towards him. He and Paul Kimber were standing by the table where the drinks were, pouring out fresh ones for themselves. They both had their backs to us and Kate, on her sofa, had closed her eyes, as if she were almost as ready as Boz to fall asleep. So Anna could talk to me more or less privately, if that was what she wanted to do.

Apparently it was, for she dropped her voice almost to a whisper.

'Yes, I can hardly believe in it yet,' she said. 'I'm not even sure if I ought to. But it's such a wonderful offer he's made and I think he means it. You see, he's been very worried about what I was going to do on my five thousand a year, and he's such a generous, understanding boy. He always was, I think. I remember how fond of him I was

when he used to come here as a child. Always helping me
in any little way he could, and so considerate. But I'm not
answering your question, am I? You wanted to know if I'd
decided what I was going to do when I leave here. Well, I
haven't exactly. I mean, not in detail. But Nick's suggested
that I should look for some really good old people's home
and have all the bills sent to him. Don't you think that's
wonderful?'

'You mean one of those awfully expensive places where
absolutely everything's done for you and you can take your
own furniture in if you want to and all that sort of thing?'
I said. 'He really means that?'

She nodded earnestly.

'And you'd be happy there?' I asked.

'What more could I want at my age?' she said. 'Sometimes they're in grand old houses in the country, old manor
houses or old parsonages, and they have their own res-
taurants and bars and libraries and sometimes even
cinemas, and there are nurses to look after you when you
get really infirm, they don't just turn you out to die like a
dog in the street. And naturally they cost the earth.'

As if the word dog had some meaning for Boz he raised
his head, then staggered slowly to his feet.

'It does sound wonderful,' I said, 'only somehow it's very
difficult to imagine you in a place like that. You've always
been so independent. Are you sure you'd be happy?'

'Can you suggest anything better? I couldn't get a new
job at my age, and the alternative is scraping along on my
five thousand and my old age pension in some wretched
little bedsitting-room, or perhaps going into one of those
so-called old people's homes which are really just run by
some couple who are letting out a few rooms in their own
house and which you sometimes hear such fearful things
about. I mean, sometimes when you get a bit helpless they
don't even feed you properly, or keep things clean, they just

take what they can get out of you and let you die. I know
that sort of thing isn't supposed to happen, but sometimes
it does.'

'And Nick's really offered to support you in one of the
other sort of places?' I said.

'He has, he really has.'

'Then I think that's perfectly splendid. I'm so glad.'

Boz had waddled across the room towards us and now
had laid his chin on my knee and was gazing up at me with
what struck me as a sadly appealing glance. I felt flattered
as one always does when an animal, for reasons of his own,
singles one out when there are other people about for his
attention. But Boz in the past had always shown signs of
liking me.

'And it was all Nick's own idea,' Anna went on. 'It's
really why he's going to London. He wants to fix things up
with Mr Bairnsfather so that he can start paying my bills
for me even before the will's been proved. Of course he
couldn't afford to do it out of his own present income, and
I told him there was absolutely no hurry about it because
I'll be staying on here for a while and with my savings I
can easily afford to pay for some quite good lodgings for a
time. But he said he wanted to be sure he could get it all
fixed up and that when I go into the kind of home we're
talking about, the bills can be settled on his account by Mr
Bairnsfather when he himself goes back to Australia. But
tell me something, Virginia—' She reached out and laid a
hand on my arm. 'Ought I to accept it?'

'Of course you ought,' I said. 'It's what Mrs Lovelock
meant to do for you, I'm sure, before she got too absent-
minded to rewrite her will.'

'But he's so young and he may get married and have a
family and find I'm an absolute millstone round his neck.
And if he wanted to stop paying my bills then, when I'm
older than I am now, I'd find it much harder to adjust to a

change than if I settled into something quite cheap straight away.'

'Won't there be a contract of some sort?'

'I don't know. I hadn't thought of that. He hasn't said anything about it and I don't like the idea of raising it, as if I didn't trust him.'

'I'm sure Mr Bairnsfather will raise it, if Nick doesn't.'

'You really think so?'

'What are lawyers for, after all? Incidentally, is Kate taking part in this?'

'I don't really know. I don't think so. She hasn't mentioned it, and naturally I don't like to raise the subject myself.'

'Is there any special place you know of where you'd like to go?'

'Well, there's Holden Dene, that lovely old house about five miles out of Allingford. You probably know it. It's got a splendid reputation and if I went there I could keep in touch with all my Allingford friends. But perhaps one has to go on a waiting-list to get in. I really don't know. And if I couldn't go there, I'm sure I could find somewhere else. But I told you, my head's in a whirl. It's all so surprising. It's the very last thing I'd been thinking of.'

Boz had moved closer to me and was prodding me with his cold nose, wanting more attention than he was getting from me. I started to stroke his head and all of a sudden had an extraordinary impulse.

'Anna, I came here today to choose something of Mrs Lovelock's and I've got my photograph of her and the puppies,' I said, 'but could I take Boz too? You won't be able to take him to Holden Dene.'

She looked as startled as I was myself by my words.

'Take him with you? Take him now, d'you mean?' she said.

'Well, no, I suppose I couldn't actually do that,' I

replied. 'I'd have to lay in some supplies of food for him and get him a basket to sleep in and all that, though I suppose you could let me take his old one in the car. But I'd have to get a bit organized. I could pick him up in a day or two, though.'

She gave a little shake of her head. 'I'd think it over, if I were you. I know why you made the suggestion and I feel the same. I've always been very fond of him and I hate to face the fact that he's coming to the end of his days. But he's almost there anyway, poor dear. He's very old.'

'All right, I'll think it over,' I said. 'But I did mean it.'

'Of course you did. But a dog's quite a lot of trouble, you know, anyway in a town. It's different if you've got fields all round you and you can turn him loose. Not that there are many places where you can do that nowadays, I imagine, what with traffic what it is, even on country roads.'

I agreed, already rather grateful that she had not immediately taken me up on my offer. It had been more than a little crazy, I was beginning to think. I had only a very small garden, not a quarter the size of Mrs Lovelock's, and Ellsworthy Street was fairly busy. So if I took Boz home with me I should somehow have to persuade the postman, the milkman, the laundryman and the newspaper boy to shut my gate behind them when they called instead of leaving it, as they usually did, standing open, or else he would be a prisoner in the house and he would be alone a good deal of the time while I was out at work. I would of course take him for a walk mornings and evenings, but I did not know how soon I would get tired of doing that. Anna was right, he would be a good deal of trouble.

As a child, living in a quiet country spot, I had had a dog to whom I had been devoted and who, it happened, had had a good deal of influence on my later life. My parents had never taught me anything about religion and my first encounter with it had been when I went to school.

At first I had been inclined to be impressed, but then someone had told me that my dog had no soul and therefore
could not go to heaven and this had seemed to me a pretty
poor look-out. I cared for him a good deal more than for
most of the people I knew, so the attractions of the creed
that I was being taught had soon waned. Looking at Boz
now and meeting his sad, earnest eyes, I wondered if he
really had no soul. It seemed to me that he must have at
least as much of one as I had myself.

I repeated, 'I'll think it over, but I'm sure I'll call for
him in a day or two.'

And to my own surprise, I meant it.

'Of course there's no hurry about it,' Anna said. 'No
one's putting him into the street, any more than they are
me. People can be very kind to us old things. Not that it's
everyone who's got someone like Nick to think for them.
You really feel I ought to let him do what he suggested?'

'I shouldn't hesitate for a moment,' I said.

Kate had just got up from her sofa and came to join us.

'You two look very serious,' she said, dropping on to a
stool near Anna. 'What have you been talking about?'

'About Boz,' Anna said. 'Virginia's just offered to take
him.'

'That's a very noble offer,' Kate said. 'Take him now, do
you mean? Nick would be so glad if you did.'

'I've told her she should think it over,' Anna replied. 'She
just hates the thought of him being put down.'

'And Nick can't wait to have it done,' Kate said. 'He
hates him, you know. He pretends he's outgrown his fear
of dogs, but you can see him go tense every time Boz goes
near him. He was savaged by one of Aunt Helen's dogs
when he was a child and some people never outgrow that
sort of thing.'

I remembered that she had referred to something of the
sort when she and Nick had met on the day of the funeral.

'That's absolute nonsense,' Anna said impatiently. 'No one could be afraid of Boz now, though he was a fine, upstanding young fellow when he was young. That was why Helen kept him when she got rid of the other dogs. It's a breed that can be savage, of course, if they aren't properly trained. She used to have to keep them very carefully under control.'

'And you really think Nick isn't afraid of him?' Kate said. There was something sardonic in her tone. 'You like Nick so much, don't you, Anna?'

'And you don't,' I said.

She raised her eyebrows. 'I'm not sure . . .' The mocking note had suddenly gone from her voice and the sentence sounded unfinished. 'If I could be really sure . . .' But she left that uncompleted too and got up and walked away.

Later I was to remember that uncertainty of hers.

'Well, I must be going,' I said and stood up. 'And I'll let you know about Boz tomorrow, Anna.'

She smiled up at me. 'Don't get carried away by the idea, just out of generosity. Give yourself longer than that.'

I said goodbye to the two men and let myself out.

The evening had become a little foggy and I drove home slowly. I thought about Boz as I went, wondering if he would actually be happy if I took him to live with me. Perhaps he was old enough not to care much about where he was. One place might be as good as another to him so long as he was fed and kept warm. On the other hand, might he not be unable to settle contentedly into unfamiliar surroundings and be scared by all the time that he would have to spend by himself? I began to feel fairly sure that my suggestion had been a very stupid one, just a salve to my own sentimentality and not of much good to the poor old creature. I might even find I was having to have him put down quite soon. Anna had been right to insist that I should think it over.

Reaching home, I locked the car away in the garage and let myself into the house. There was some stew that I could warm up for my supper and a half-empty bottle of Côtes du Rhône that came from the supermarket. I put them on a tray and took them into the sitting-room and sat down by the gas fire, which I lit for the sake of the glow that it gave, rather than because the room felt cold. I put the photograph of Mrs Lovelock that I had brought home with me on the mantelpiece, not intending to leave it there, but because for the moment it was the easiest thing to do with it. I thought that in the end I would very likely put it away in a drawer. I have never much cared for having photographs around me.

I possessed one of Felix, but that I kept in a drawer, feeling that there would be a sort of brutality about throwing it away and yet that it would be intolerable to have it where I could see it. Anyway, it was of a Felix much younger than he was now. Its smile had the boyish charm that had lasted him into his thirties but which he had long outgrown and it hardly hinted at the air of distinction that he had later acquired. An air that was entirely misleading, because he was not distinguished in anything. Such talents as he might have had if he had ever attempted to cultivate them had been wholly wasted. Even as the crook and the con-man that he was, he was strictly small-time.

I did not know how he was earning a living at the moment, but somehow he was managing to make enough to scrape along in the flat in Little Carbery Street, a very minor street in Bloomsbury where we had spent the three years of our marriage. And he ran a car, no doubt picked up cheaply through some dubious connection that he had made during the time when he had worked as a salesman in a second-hand car dearler's, whose managing director happened to be in gaol for fraud. In those days, when I had still believed in him, I had thought that he was a civil engineer, working for a big construction firm, only to discover by chance that they had never even heard of him. That had been the beginning of my disillusionment, though even now, even when I thought I knew all that there was to know about him, I could not quite get out of the way of feeling a certain fondness for him. But his photograph stayed in a drawer. I did not look at it from one year's end to the other.

After I had had my supper I turned on the television for a while and watched a wild life programme, one of the few things they ever show that I enjoy, and after it I started on the news. But it had been on for only a few minutes when the telephone rang. I switched off the television and lifted the telephone. It was Paul Kimber. He asked me a curious question.

'Virginia, would you be inclined to say that I am a fairly honest person?' he asked.

'I've no evidence to the contrary,' I answered.

'If I told you something, even something rather strange, you'd be inclined to believe me?' he said.

'I suppose it would depend on just how strange it was, Paul,' I said. 'Some people who seem the most stable you've ever met turn out to have the most extraordinary beliefs and superstitions. It isn't that they aren't honest. They really do believe in these things.'

'It isn't a case of belief or superstition, it's a very simple matter of fact. And I'd like your advice on what I ought to do.'

'I don't mind giving you some then, so long as I feel fairly sure you won't take it. I'd hate to feel responsible for what you may do. What's the problem?'

'It's about Mrs Lovelock's emeralds. You've seen them, haven't you?'

'Yes, I saw them when Nick took them out of the safe to show to Kate that afternoon after the funeral.'

'And what did you think of them?'

I remembered how uneasy Paul seemed to have become when the emeralds were shown.

'That they were very fine, I suppose,' I said, 'though you'd have to have a good deal of courage to wear them.'

'But nothing about them struck you as—strange?'

'No. Should it?'

'Perhaps not, if you aren't an expert. But you know I had the clasp mended recently for Mrs Lovelock?'

'Yes, I remember you saying so.'

'Well, I did, and when she gave them to me I discovered something distinctly strange about them. There isn't an emerald among them. They're all fakes.'

'Fakes!' I exclaimed.

'I'm no expert myself, of course,' he went on, 'but I spotted it pretty quickly, and that's why I didn't mend the clasp at home. I could easily have done it, but I thought I'd sooner have a witness to the fact that I hadn't done any tampering with the things, so I took them up to London, to Elvis and Co. in Bond Street and of course they spotted the fakes at once and there's a statement of that on the receipt they gave me. "To repairing clasp of imitation emerald necklace . . ." They were not a little interested in how I'd come by the things and said it had been a remarkably good job when it was done and probably quite expensive, though nowhere near the value of the original gems.'

'And you told all this to Mrs Lovelock?'

'No, I didn't, you see.'

'Why ever not?'

'I didn't want to upset her. She obviously believed the things were genuine and I didn't know how she'd got them herself. I mean, had her husband given them to her, or had she inherited them from a parent or someone? And as they just stayed in her safe and there was no risk that she might think of selling them, or anything like that, I didn't see what harm it could do if she went on thinking they were the real thing.'

'And why are you worried about that now?'

'Because of course they'll have to be valued for probate, now she's dead. There are some people coming in to start on the job one day soon, and they'll spot the trouble at once. And people are going to remember that I had the necklace in my possession for a time only recently, and even though I've got that receipt, things may get unpleasant. Once a suspicion gets going, it can sometimes be very difficult to get rid of it completely, even in spite of the evidence.'

'Yes, I see.' I thought about it for a moment. 'What I'm not sure of, Paul, is why you've come to me for advice. I don't know the first thing about precious stones.'

'No, but you do know me,' he said. 'And I know your ex-husband and I realized you've had some experience of spotting things that—well, that don't ring quite true, if you see what I mean.'

I never call Felix my ex-husband, because of our never having troubled to get a divorce, but I did not correct him.

'I see exactly what you mean,' I said.

'Now don't get annoyed with me, please,' he said. 'I really would like to know if you think what I've just told you is true.'

'At the moment I'm inclined to believe you absolutely,' I said. 'I nearly always believe everything that anybody tells me. My doubts, if they arise, always creep in little by little some time later. But really I think I do believe you, Paul.'

'And what do you think I ought to do about it?'

That was a question that I had seen coming and to which I had no answer ready.

'Have you told this to anyone else yet?' I asked.

'No.'

'Then I'd tell it at least to Nick and Kate, and of course

to Anna, because she's the one who knows you best and can vouch for your character.'

'Will you vouch for my character, if you're asked about me?'

'Oh yes, certainly. Not that we really know each other so very well.'

He gave an ironic laugh. 'There you are, you see! Even you don't want to commit yourself definitely. It if gets around that I'm a thief and a forger, you'll say you've always had certain doubts about me. I'm not sure I wouldn't have certain doubts about myself, if I were someone else. I live in a way that a lot of people think odd and I think some of them wonder where I get my money from. Actually, my family used to own land in Yorkshire and selling it left me quite well off. I don't really need to earn anything.'

'I shouldn't worry too much about it, Paul,' I said. 'For one thing, I know you make some pretty jewellery, but have you really got the skill to do the sort of job that must have been done on Mrs Lovelock's necklace?'

'Ah, that's the best defence I've got,' he said with another laugh. 'Of course I haven't. Any expert would vouch for that, I suppose. Well, thank you for listening to me, Virginia. Just talking about it has made me feel that my fears are just a silly sort of nightmare. See you again sometime soon, I hope.'

He rang off.

I went up to bed early that evening and going to the window in my bedroom to draw the curtains, saw that the fog had thickened considerably. Where the light from the window fell on it, it looked like a heavy white blanket hung against the glass. The little traffic that there was in the road went crawling by, the headlights hardly showing. I drew the curtains, got into bed and for a little while read a thriller that I had recently got from the library, but I soon switched off my light and almost at once was asleep.

When I woke at about half past seven it seemed to me that I had spent most of the night dreaming, yet I could not remember just what had happened in any of my dreams. In the same way, I found it difficult to remember much about the day before, though I had a feeling that something of importance had happened. But I could not think what it was until I suddenly remembered my offer to adopt Boz. Well, of course, having made the offer, I should have to stick to it. Since coming to live in Ellsworthy Street I had never once thought of keeping a pet, but as I got up, put on my dressing-gown and went downstairs to make coffee for breakfast, I found myself liking the idea very much. I decided to let Anna know sometime that day that my mind was quite made up about it.

But it never happened.

At soon after nine o'clock the telephone rang and it was Anna.

'Virginia, I must see you please as soon as possible,' she gasped, her voice shaking. 'Something terrible has happened. It's Kate. Can you believe it, I found her dead in bed this morning and she'd been shot? Yes, I said shot. Right through her heart. And what's so awful too, they've taken Nick in for questioning. Nick! They actually think he could have done it. And Boz is dead too and they think he was poisoned. And here I am, all alone. Oh, please, please, Virginia, come as soon as you can. I've a very special reason for asking for you.'

CHAPTER 4

I gulped some more coffee, dressed as quickly as I could, got into my car and drove out to Morebury Close. I had not even begun to take in what Anna had told me. The fog of the evening before had gone and a wind was blowing. It felt colder, more autumnal than it had yet that year. Dead leaves, in the teeth of the wind, blew against my windscreen.

As I turned into the Close an ambulance drove out of it. I felt a sharp shiver as I thought of what was probably inside it, yet I could not understand what had happened. Why had anyone wanted to shoot Kate, and in her bed too? If burglars had broken in and she had surprised them so that they had shot her in panic, would she not have been lying on the floor somewhere, perhaps in the drawing-room, or the kitchen or possibly even in her bedroom, but not in her bed? And who could have poisoned Boz?

I began to wonder if Anna had told me the facts correctly, or if she had been in such a state of shock that she had been quite confused.

There were several police cars in front of Mrs Lovelock's bungalow and a number of people gathered in the street outside, the news of murder somehow already having reached them and drawn them there to stare and listen and speculate. When I tried to turn in at the gate a uniformed constable stepped out and stopped me.

I told him that I was Mrs Freer and that I was a friend of Miss Cox.

'She telephoned and asked me to come,' I said. 'Can't I go in?'

'You're aware of what's happened, then?' he said.

'I know what she's told me.'

'Mrs Freer, you said?' He had a portable radio in his hand. He spoke to it. 'A Mrs Freer is here, says Miss Cox asked her to come, sir. All right if I let her in?'

He seemed to receive some answer, for he stood aside and waved me on. I drove as near to the door as I could, parking behind one of the police cars there, got out and went to the front door of the bungalow. Another policeman there wanted to know who I was and when I told him, showed me into the dining-room, where I did not find Anna, but two men, both of whom I recognized. They recognized me too, though they did not give any sign that this gave them any satisfaction.

'Good morning,' one of them said. 'We meet again.'

It was Detective-Superintendent Dawnay, whom I had met on several occasions. He was about forty-five, a thickset man, not as tall as policemen usually are, with dark brown hair and unusually dark skin which made his light grey eyes look almost colourless. They were intelligent yet expressionless, as if he liked to keep his intelligence to himself. The other man was Detective-Sergeant Wells, tall and burly and as I remembered him, given to silence, at least when his senior officer was present.

'Sit down, Mrs Freer,' the superintendent said. 'There are just a few things you may be able to tell us. First, Miss Cox asked you to come, did she?'

'Yes,' I said. I took one of the chairs at the table, but the two men remained standing.

'You're a close friend of hers, then?' Dawnay asked.

'Fairly close.'

'Had she any special reason for asking you to come, rather than any other of her friends?'

'I don't know. She said on the telephone that she had a special reason, but I don't know what it was. She sounded rather hysterical.'

He nodded. 'She's very upset. She found the body, you know.'

'And it was Kate Galvin?' I felt that I had to check what Anna had told me.

'Yes, as I understand it, a grand-niece of Mrs Helen Lovelock, who died recently.'

'That's correct. And you've arrested Mrs Lovelock's grand-nephew, Nicholas Duffield.'

'No, no, taken him in for questioning. We certainly haven't brought any charge yet.'

'But wasn't he in London yesterday evening? Hasn't he a complete alibi?'

'Actually, no. We've been told he set off for London, but turned back because of the fog. Now tell me something, Mrs Freer. I believe you were here yesterday afternoon.'

'In the late afternoon, or you might call it early evening,' I answered. 'It was around six o'clock, I think.'

He nodded again, as if that confirmed something.

'And who else was here at the time, can you tell me?'

'As far as I can remember . . .' I hesitated, my mind going blank as it often does when I am asked a direct question. 'When I arrived Mrs Bordman was here. Mrs Julia Bordman.' I almost said Mrs Bordman and Charlie, because they were so seldom apart that it would have felt like speaking of one person, but I stopped myself in time. 'Then presently Mr Kimber came in. He lives next door. Perhaps you've already seen him this morning.'

'Not yet,' Dawnay replied. 'He telephoned when he saw us arrive and we'll be going over to see him shortly. And that's all?'

'Of course Miss Galvin and Mr Duffield were here,' I said, 'and presently Mr and Mrs Roderick Hearn arrived. He's a lecturer on economics at the Polytechnic. They also live in Morebury Close.'

He glanced at some notes that he was holding.

'Yes, that's what I've been told by Miss Cox. And just why were you all here? It isn't altogether usual to hold parties so soon after funerals.'

'It wasn't exactly a party. Just a few people were asked who'd known Mrs Lovelock fairly well, to see if we'd each like some memento of her. I took a photograph of her, standing among some puppies. You know she used to breed Staffordshire bull terriers until she got too old to go on with it.'

'So I've been told,' he said.

'And that reminds me . . .'

'Yes?' he said as I hesitated again.

'She kept a dog, a very old dog, and there'd been some talk of him having to be put down when the house was sold and Miss Cox went away. But when she telephoned this morning she said that he was dead.'

'That's right.'

'And she said you think he'd been poisoned.'

'It's a possibility. It'll have to be investigated.'

'Where was he?'

'In the kitchen.'

'But why on earth should anyone kill poor old Boz? He was utterly harmless.'

'He could still bark, couldn't he?'

That was true, of course. Boz had had a fairly fierce and noisy bark.

'But if there was no one in the house to wake but Miss Cox and Miss Galvin . . .' Then another thought struck me. 'Why didn't the sound of the shot wake Miss Cox? She told me she only found Miss Galvin this morning.'

'It seems she takes sleeping-pills every night,' he answered. 'Sleeping-pills with a mug of hot milk. And she told me when she's taken them she can sleep through even a violent thunderstorm.'

'So even if Boz had barked, it wouldn't have woken her.'

'So she claims.'

'So why did he have to be killed? . . . Oh, it was by someone who didn't know Nick Duffield was going to be in London last night. Only you say he wasn't. But they didn't know he wouldn't be, did they? It was only by chance that he came back. Or do you think . . . ?' I was beginning to understand, I thought, what the superintendent was thinking, though I felt muddled. 'You don't believe it was by chance he came back, you think he intended to do that all along, and the fog just kept him here. What time did he get in?'

'About eleven o'clock, he says.'

'And when was Miss Galvin killed?'

'You know I can't tell you that offhand,' he said. 'We'll have to wait for what the forensic people have to say.'

'Yes, of course. But could it have been before eleven?'

'We think it could have been.'

'Or later?'

'Not much later.'

'I see.' Not that I really saw very much, except that his pale grey eyes were no longer interested in me, in fact that he was beginning to feel that he had told me more than I had told him and that that was not what he had intended. I stood up.

'I can see Miss Cox, can I?' I said.

'Certainly, if she wants to see you.'

'Where is she?'

'I believe in her bedroom. Our people are in the drawing-room and the kitchen and of course in Miss Galvin's room, though the photographers have done their job and she's been taken away. I'm afraid you'll find the old lady in a very distressed state. Do you know if she was particularly attached to Miss Galvin?'

'I don't really know,' I answered. 'But walking in on a

murder is liable to distress anybody, isn't it, if they aren't used to it?'

I was profoundly thankful that I should not have to view the body.

'Yes, indeed,' he said with a wry smile and I found myself wondering how much distress he felt himself when that was what he had to do. Perhaps more than he was inclined to show, though in a place like Allingford it might not be something that happened to him so very often. Grievous bodily harm, sexual assaults, drugs, driving over the limit, burglaries, those might all be in the day's work, but cold-blooded murder was another thing.

And the murder of Kate Galvin, shot through the heart while she lay in her bed, must surely have been as cold-blooded as murder could be. There were many more questions that I might have asked him, but I knew that he wanted to be rid of me and I left the room and went looking for Anna.

I had never been in her room, but I knew which it was. I knocked on the door, but heard no response. Knocking again and again hearing nothing, I opened the door a little way and said softly, 'It's Virginia, Anna. Can I come in?'

'Virginia! Yes, yes, come in!'

As I opened the door wider I saw her come trotting across the room towards me, and found myself held tight in her arms, crushed against her short, sturdy body.

'Oh, thank you for coming! It's so awful, being alone here now that they've taken Nick away. Can you imagine it?—Nick! That dear, generous boy. And I've never been really alone in my life before, isn't that extraordinary? That's something I've never thought about before. One doesn't think of such a thing until it happens to one.'

She had hauled me into the room and shut the door. I should not have said that she was alone in the house, in fact I had never seen it so full of people, most of them rather large, quiet men who seemed to be too busy with their own affairs to take any notice of my presence, but I knew what she meant.

'Even Boz!' she said, still clutching me as if I gave her some feeling of balance. 'Even Boz has gone. Helen, Kate, Nick, Boz . . . Oh, come and sit down and have some coffee. I've been drinking it to try and steady my nerves, but there's still some left.'

She manœuvred me into a chair by the window and gave me a cup of coffee. The window overlooked the garden at the back of the bungalow, most of which was lawn with the sheds which were the old disused dog-kennels at the end of it. There was a silver birch near the house, its leaves now splendidly golden, and a rose-bed which still had a few late-blooming blossoms on the bushes.

The room itself was square and not very large and was very neat. In spite of all that must have happened that morning, Anna had found time to make the bed, which was covered with a cream-coloured candlewick bedspread, but considering for how many years she must have occupied the room, there were very few purely personal things there. A purple quilted nylon dressing-gown hung from a peg on the door and a pair of purple velvet bedroom slippers had been placed carefully side by side by the bed. There was a handsome old-fashioned set of silver-backed brush, comb and mirror on the dressing-table, perhaps a present from Mrs Lovelock, and there was a small bookcase filled with paperbacks, most of them romantic novels. The only pictures on the walls were photographs of dogs. There was the cretonne-covered chair in which I had sat down and a chair at the dressing-table which Anna pulled round to sit on herself, facing me. On a coffee table between us was a tray with a coffee-pot on it and two cups, which showed that she had been expecting me.

'Anna, I don't understand anything,' I said. 'That man Dawnay has told me a certain amount, but he hasn't told me why they think Nick may have killed Kate. Because they do, don't they?'

She nodded sombrely, her heavy features grim.

'Oh yes, they do,' she said. 'They call it taking him in for inquiries, but they wouldn't have done that if they weren't suspicious, would they?'

'But why are they suspicious? What's his motive supposed to have been?

'Money, of course. With Kate dead, he'll get the lot, won't he? And then there's the poisoning of Boz.'

'To stop him barking?'

She nodded again. 'They think Nick's setting off for London was just a blind to set up an alibi and it wasn't because of the fog that he turned back, but it was the fog that kept him here after the murder, which wasn't what he'd intended. He'd meant to come back quite soon after setting out, knowing I'd have taken my sleeping-pills and probably wouldn't wake up and that if Boz didn't bark Kate wouldn't wake up either when he came in. And then, when he'd killed her, he could really start off again for London and claim he'd got there earlier than he did. But with the fog as thick as it was for a time and with his not knowing the road, he didn't dare set out but stayed on here. And he smashed a window in the kitchen to make it look as if someone got in that way, and then when he was questioned this morning he claimed the murder must have happened during the time he was out, because if it had happened later he'd have heard the shot.'

'But why do they think he had to kill Boz?' I asked. 'Boz knew him. Would he have barked when he came back to the house?'

'I'm afraid he might have,' Anna replied. 'He'd sometimes bark even at me if he wasn't expecting me. He really got very nervous in his old age. So that's no defence. And what's so against Nick is that if they're right that Boz was poisoned, then whatever he was given must have been put into the dish in which I'd put his supper in the kitchen, or perhaps in his drinking-water. They've taken both bowls away to be examined. And of course they've taken Boz and they're going to cut him open. But in any case, if he was really poisoned and didn't simply happen to die a natural death, which is actually possible at his age, it could only have been done by someone who was in the house yesterday. And that means Nick or me.'

'Now wait a moment,' I said. 'I don't think they've absolutely made up their minds about that. One of the things the superintendent asked me was who had been in the house earlier in the evening. He didn't tell me why he wanted to know, but I told him Paul Kimber had been here, and Julia Bordman and the Hearns. But don't you think he was trying to find out if anyone besides you and Nick could have got at Boz's supper?'

She gave me a doubting look, as if she wanted to discern how seriously I meant what I had said and whether or not there was any comfort in it for her.

Then she said uncertainly, 'I suppose . . . Yes, I never thought of that . . . I suppose one of them could have done it. I must try to remember if any of them could have got out to the kitchen without my seeing them. I was coming and going so much, so perhaps they could. It's just possible —yes, I'm sure it's possible!' Her face lit up. 'I knew I was right to ask you to come to me!'

'You said you had a special reason for asking me to come,' I said. 'What was it?'

'Oh, it was because I thought you might be able to get your husband to come down to help Nick,' she answered. 'He was so clever, wasn't he, finding out who killed Miss

Dale—Imogen Dale, wasn't that her name?* I heard all about it from that nice girl, Meg Randall, who ended up marrying one of the policemen who'd been on the case. Do you think as a very special favour you could persuade Felix to come to Allingford?'

She was quite right about Felix being clever. He can be very clever, though if ever a person has wasted his natural talents, it is Felix. It is not everyone who realizes how many he has.

'Of course I could ask him,' I said, 'but I don't know much about what he's doing at the moment.' If she had been offering him a fee as a private investigator I was sure there would be no difficulty in persuading him to come, but that did not seem to have occurred to her and I did not like to raise the matter myself. 'Just what do you want him to do?'

'To find out who really killed Kate, of course,' she said, 'and to clear Nick. I know you may think I'm just being selfish. He promised to pay my expenses in a really good old people's home and I dare say he wouldn't be able to do that, even if he wanted to, if he was in prison. I don't know much about that sort of thing. But that really isn't why I'm so worried about him. It's because I've got so fond of him during the short time he's been here and he's already had so much tragedy in his life with his parents dying as they did, that this seems so appallingly—oh, so appallingly unfair. Why should he have to endure it?'

'Don't you think the police will arrive at the truth?'

'Perhaps they will. I know that man Dawnay seems quite intelligent. But look at what they're saying about the emeralds.'

* _Last Will and Testament._

'The emeralds?' I was startled. 'They didn't say anything about emeralds to me.'

'Didn't they? Well, almost the first thing they did when they got here was to ask me where Helen kept her valuables, so I showed them the safe—it happened I hadn't been into the drawing-room yet this morning—and it was open. Wide open! And the emeralds had gone. But instead of taking for granted, as sensible people would, that the theft was the motive for the murder, they started nodding and muttering to one another and being very mysterious. Oh, why do people have to try to be mysterious and subtle instead of accepting the obvious? They think, you see, like Nick's setting off for London, it may have been simply a blind, and that's simply because they'd already made up their minds that he was the murderer, and he'd no need to steal the emeralds because he'd get their value anyway. What they think is that he took them because he wanted to make things look as if the murderer came in from outside, which, as I was telling you, they don't believe because of Boz being poisoned by someone who must have been inside the house at some time.'

'And what do they think Nick did with the emeralds?'

I was thinking about Paul Kimber's telephone call to me and what he had told me about the necklace. If Dawnay had told me about the emeralds being missing, I probably would have told him about the call, but now I was not at all sure what I ought to do. I was inclined to leave it to Paul himself to tell them what he chose. They would certainly get around to questioning him presently and I had begun to have a strange, uneasy idea that it was just possible that Paul had not told me the truth.

He had asked me very insistently if I believed him and until this moment I had done so without question, but now everything seemed different. The safe was open and the necklace was missing and there had been a murder and perhaps Paul actually wanted me to tell the police about that call of his, just because the stones were in fact not a fake, and he only wanted them to think so, so that he of all people could have had no apparent motive for stealing them. But if I tried to tell any of this to Anna she was likely to say that I was being too subtle for her, and I was inclined to think that probably I was.

She was looking particularly grim. 'What do they think Nick did with them? And what do they think he did with the gun? Just ask them that, will you? Of course they haven't the faintest idea.'

'Because if he really shot Kate and helped himself to the emeralds they can't be far away, can they? If he really didn't drive out into the fog he must have hidden them somewhere fairly near.'

'Exactly. And they've begun searching. I got them to begin with this room so that I could have it to myself when they'd done and I could have a little peace. And I must say they were most careful, although they were very thorough. There was very little tidying I had to do when they'd gone. I don't know where they are now—in the drawing-room, I think.'

'Had the safe been broken open, or was it done by some-one who knew the combination?' I asked.

'It hadn't been broken open,' she said. 'It looks as if someone did know the combination. But quite a number of people knew it, you know, besides Nick. I do myself. I could open it as easily as I can the fridge. And Paul Kimber knows it and I wouldn't be surprised if Julia Bordman does too. Helen's having a safe was really ridiculous. It was a sort of pretence. When she wanted to show off her treasures to someone she'd stay in her chair by the fire and get them to open the safe for her and bring her over the cases inside it and then put them back again and close it.'

'Was anything else taken besides the emeralds?'

'I don't think so.'

'Talking of Julia . . .'

'Yes?' Anna said as I paused.

I was not sure what I had been about to say, but after a moment I went on. 'She was here yesterday without Charlie. I believe it's the very first time I've seen her without him.'

'Yes, I know.'

'Why was that, do you know? I mean, why wasn't he with her?'

It was Anna who now took some time to answer, then she gave a shrug of her shoulders and said, 'I don't know. Perhaps he wasn't well.'

'I shouldn't have thought she'd have come if he wasn't well,' I said.

'No, I suppose not.' She hesitated again, drinking the last of the coffee in her cup. 'So you don't know the old story,' she said at length.

'I don't think I know any old story about the Bordmans,' I said.

'I don't much like talking about it. It isn't a nice story.'

'About Charlie?'

'Yes.'

'Well, we all know he isn't exactly normal, but he seems harmless enough.'

'Seems so, yes.'

'Well, if you don't want to tell me the story, don't,' I said.

That seemed to be the way to spur her on to tell it.

'It's because of Kate, you see,' she said. 'Julia only agreed to bring him here after the funeral because Kate wasn't here. You may have noticed that when Kate walked in later Julia took him away as quickly as possible. I wouldn't have thought myself that after all this time Kate would have recognized him, but one could see at once that she did. In a way I was surprised that Julia risked taking him to the funeral because she couldn't have known that Kate wouldn't be there, but I suppose she thought it was safe when there were sure to be so many other people there and that she'd be able to keep them apart. And Charlie was always very fond of Helen.'

'But what had Kate done to him?'

'It's what he did to her. She must have been about ten years old and she was staying here with Helen and seemed to be such good friends with Charlie, who was still just like a child himself, then one day he assaulted her—sexually, I mean. I don't think he actually got as far as raping her, but it wasn't far off, and it seems she's never forgotten it.'

I had a sharp feeling of revulsion and Anna must have seen it, for she added, 'I told you it wasn't a nice story.'

'But what happened?' I asked. 'I mean, weren't the police called in?'

She shook her head. 'People weren't as open about that sort of thing then as they are now. And it was thought that any publicity might do Kate more harm than good. She was terribly frightened and distressed, and I suppose it's possible that being questioned by the police and all that would only have made things worse for her. Anyway, Julia pleaded with Helen not to hand Charlie over to them. She begged and pleaded. She promised that if Helen would say nothing about what had happened she'd get Charlie into a psychiatric hospital and she did that and he was there for quite a long time. And you've seen how things are now that he's home. Julia's completely given up her life to looking after him. It cost her her marriage and I've always felt terribly sorry for her. To be honest with you, I don't really like her very much. It's difficult to like a person who's so completely wrapped up in one thing. But I do admire her.'

'And Charlie's supposed to be completely cured, is he?'

'Is someone like Charlie ever cured?'

'I mean of his sexual aberrations.'

'One hopes so.'

'But you aren't sure?'

'How can one be? If Julia was absolutely sure herself, would she keep quite such a close watch on him? But in his way he's such a nice creature, isn't he? Sad and pathetic, of course, but always gentle and good-mannered. And he can't help being what he is.'

'But you think that when Kate suddenly came face to face with him after the funeral, she was really frightened of him?'

'For a moment I think she was. And later that evening, when you'd all gone, I tried to get her to talk about it because I'd some idea in my head that that was the right thing to do. I mean, that it's healthier that things like that shouldn't be buried. But perhaps I was wrong, or anyway went the wrong way about it, because she only began to laugh at me, as it it had all been a great joke, and let me see that she thought me a silly old fool to be thinking about it at all, as perhaps I was.'

'But Julia didn't bring him here yesterday afternoon,' I said.

'No.'

'However, I don't see what all that can have to do with what happened to Kate last night.'

'I suppose not.'

'Anna, why do you think there could have been some connection?'

She waited a moment, then she shook her head.

'Wasn't it you who brought it up?' she said. 'You started talking about Julia. I didn't even want to tell you the story.'

That was true and I started trying to remember why I had really wanted to talk about Julia. It had not been only because I had been curious about her having come to the house without Charlie. There had been something else in my mind. Then I realized that it was because of Boz. Julia was one of the people who just conceivably could have put the poison in his food in the kitchen. As she had been leaving she had been by herself in the hall for a minute or two while Anna had taken the Hearns into the dining-room to look for their memento of Helen, and then if Julia had been very swift and very determined about it, she might have darted into the kitchen, dropped the poison into the dog's dish, then let herself out.

But that would have to mean, of course, not only that she had made up her mind beforehand to return later, so that she had to be sure of silencing him, but also that she knew where the dish was likely to be and that it might already have his supper in it. That seemed extremely unlikely. The whole idea was absurd.

'Talking of old stories,' I said, 'do you know the truth of what happened between Kate and Roderick Hearn?'

Anna gave an abrupt laugh. 'You're really trying, aren't you, Virginia? You do want to find all the suspects you can. I'm very grateful to you and Nick should be grateful too.'

'I was just thinking that if I'm to ask Felix to come down to solve the murder,' I said, 'the more I can tell him the better.'

'You're really going to ask him, then?'

'Oh, I'll ask him. And my guess is, he'll come. But I shouldn't like to make any promises for him. About Roderick and Kate. They were engaged once, weren't they?'

Her forehead wrinkled as she seemed to be trying to remember. 'I don't really know so very much about it. I believe it was Roderick and Margot who were engaged, with the date of the wedding fixed and everything, then Kate came down to stay with Helen and suddenly the wedding was called off and Roderick disappeared, and it just happened that Kate disappeared at the same time, and there was a lot of gossip locally. But Margot said it was she

who'd broken the engagement because Roderick was trying
to interfere with her career, and actually it was about
another year before they got married. Not that she'd really
got a career yet. It was only later she took to writing, though
now, as you know, she's managed to produce a surprisingly
successful detective story.'

'Then actually Roderick and Kate were never engaged,
which was what I'd heard,' I said.

She gave another shrug of her shoulders. 'Oh no. And
then Kate went off to America and that seemed to be the
end of any relationship she'd ever had with Roderick. I
always assumed the two of them had had a sudden, wild
sort of love-affair which deep down didn't mean much to
either of them, and a story of their being engaged was put
about, just to try to stop Helen being too much upset about
the whole thing. Not that she was in the least upset. I think
she'd had her own affairs in her time after her husband
died. She was so attractive.'

Looking at the squat, solid old woman sitting opposite
to me, I wondered if she had had any affairs in her time,
but I found it hard to imagine. I could easily believe it of
Helen Lovelock, but Anna Cox seemed to me to be one of
those sexless beings who perhaps are really lesbians, though
they have never found this out about themselves. Certainly
in all the time that I had known her the only strong emotion
in her life had seemed to be her devotion to Mrs Lovelock.
Yet after a fashion, she seemed almost to have fallen in love
with Nick, or at least she obviously felt some strong
maternal yearning for him. The money with which he had
promised to provide her might not be the whole reason for
her anxiety about him.

'But Margot can't have been exactly pleased to see Kate,'
I said. 'In fact, from what you've told me, it sounds as if
Kate wasn't exactly a popular young woman.'

'Helen was very fond of her,' Anna said. 'But perhaps

you're right. I don't think she had many real friends. She'd attract people quite often, then somehow put them off. Look how it was with Nick. I thought when they first met they were really going to take to one another, but then something seemed to go wrong, I don't know what it was. But yesterday they were hardly speaking.'

'I met him in town, you know, the day before yesterday,' I said, 'and he told me she didn't like him. But he didn't say he didn't like her. However, people don't get murdered only because they aren't specially popular. Anna, did any other person come to the house yesterday either before I came or after I left, besides the ones we've been talking about? Remember the front door was open when I arrived.'

'Only Dr Cairns,' she said.

'He came, did he?'

'Just for a few minutes. He said he was very busy. I think that was after you'd gone.'

'It's just that I can't help wondering if anyone else came in who could have poisoned Boz, but you think not.'

'If they did, I don't know how they did it.'

'I wonder if the poison was really in one of his bowls. Couldn't he have picked it up somewhere outside? With the door open, he could have gone out by himself, couldn't he?'

'The police will be able to tell us about that later, I suppose.'

'If it really was in his supper or his drinking-water . . .'

'Yes?' she said as I stopped and stood up.

'It's just that I can't help feeling Nick is the best suspect. But perhaps I'm wrong. Anyway, I'll get in touch with Felix as soon as I can and I'll telephone to let you know what he says.'

'Thank you—thank you so much!' She stood up too and went with me to the door. 'It isn't that I expect him to work miracles, but if he'd come I somehow shouldn't feel so helpless.'

I myself would probably feel a good deal more helpless if he came than if he did not. In fact, I was hoping that there might be some reason why it was utterly impossible for him to come to Allingford just then. For instance, he might be away from London at the moment and out of reach of the telephone, or so deeply involved in some mysterious project of his own that he would refuse to tear himself away from it. I can endure and even enjoy a small amount of Felix's company, but I am very cautious about letting any situation develop in which I have to see a little too much of him. All the same, I intended to keep my promise to Anna to try to persuade him to come to visit us, and as soon as I reached my home I picked up the telephone and dialled his number.

I was rather hoping that he would not be at home, but to my disappointment the instrument at his end was picked up almost immediately.

'Freer speaking,' he said austerely.

'Felix, this is Virginia,' I said. 'I want to ask you something a little peculiar. That's to say, I think you'll think it's peculiar. I'd like you to come down to Allingford as soon as possible.'

There was a moment of silence, as if he felt stunned, as I had rather expected him to feel.

Then he said, 'You want me to come to Allingford. You're inviting me to come to Allingford?'

'Yes.'

'You—are inviting—*inviting*—me?'

'Yes. Please come, Felix.'

'My God, you must be in trouble of some sort! Are you serious?'

'Very serious. It's a question of murder, and there's a little woman here who absolutely believes you can help her. So will you come?'

'It would be too much to hope that you're that little woman, wouldn't it?'

'It would.'

'Ah well . . .' Then suddenly his tone changed and I knew what the new tone meant. It meant that he had just become the great detective, which was one of his favourite fantasies.

'My dear Virginia, of course I'll come. So glad to be of use. Give me time to pack and I'll be on my way in half an hour.'

CHAPTER 5

I telephoned Anna to tell her that Felix was coming, though I did not know quite when he would arrive. If he had done as he had promised it would have been in time for a late lunch and in case that happened I put out two steaks, ready for grilling, and the makings of a salad. But when two o'clock had passed I put the steaks back into the fridge, helped myself to some bread and cheese, made some coffee and considered telephoning him again to find out if he actually intended to come at all. But I resisted the inclination and at nearly four o'clock I heard his ring at my doorbell.

He kissed me on the cheek and came in, carrying a suitcase. I saw his car at the gate.

'Sorry,' he said. 'Sorry, sorry! I know I ought to have been here ages ago and I know I ought to have let you know that after all I couldn't come immediately. But I was so overwhelmed at having been asked to come that I didn't think ahead. And the fact was, there were things I had to cope with before I came. After all, you can't just let people down, can you? There were things I had to arrange. How are you? You're looking wonderful.'

I had never known Felix shrink from letting people down if it suited his convenience, so this time plainly it had not. As he had said that there had been things that he had had to arrange I was curious to know what they were, but thought that I could leave it till later to find out about them.

'You had lunch some time ago, I imagine,' I said, 'but would you like some coffee?'

He knew that in the circumstances it would be instant coffee, which he intensely dislikes.

'Don't trouble, don't trouble,' he said. 'Some tea presently, perhaps, when you've told me a bit about this extraordinary invitation. Do you know, I can't remember if you've ever actually asked me to come here before? I'm delighted, of course, but you can understand that I'm puzzled.'

It was not really as extraordinary as all that. We had often met since we had quietly agreed to separate and he had stayed with me several times in Allingford, even if it had not been in the first place by my invitation. But he meant to inject what drama he could into the situation.

Though I did not feel that I could be looking as wonderful as he had said I was, I thought that he himself was looking very well and somehow also unusually prosperous. The light grey suit that he was wearing had certainly come from a good tailor and like anything that comes from a good tailor nowadays, had undoubtedly cost a great deal of money. His blue and white striped shirt and his dark blue tie had an expensive look. But he had always managed to dress well, even when he seemed to have no money to do it on, and he nearly always chose to do it formally. I had never seen him in a wind-cheater, or in anything more casual than a very luxurious-looking cashmere sweater.

He looked his age, which was in the late forties, but was carrying his years with increasing distinction. He was still, in his fashion, a very good-looking man. He had not put on any weight or developed a paunch, but was as straight and slender as ever, was of medium height and had fair hair and very bright blue eyes which had oddly drooping lids that made them look almost triangular. His whole face was more or less triangular, broad at the temples, pointed at the chin. It was a face that you would remember even if you had happened to encounter him only briefly and by chance. There had been a time when it had had a devastating effect on me.

Sitting down by my gas fire, he immediately took a packet of cigarettes out of a pocket, lit one and, leaning back in his chair, inhaling deeply, observed, 'It's nice to be here.'

Nothing would cure him of being a chain-smoker. Lung cancer and heart disease, he seemed assured, were things that happened to other people, though at times, when we had argued about it, I wondered if he could care very much if they happened to him. Under his usual cheerfulness and charm, I had sometimes felt, there was something that was deeply pessimistic and self-destructive. But perhaps I was completely mistaken about that, trying to see more than was really there, and he smoked as he did only for the simple reason that he liked it.

'I suppose you're wondering what kept me,' he said. 'Why I was so late. What could possibly have delayed me when you'd mentioned a murder and said you wanted my help? Well, the fact is, I'm helping to run a firm of cleaning-ladies—most of whom, incidentally, are men—we clean private houses, offices, hotels, you name it, we do it —and I had to find someone to take over my job of organizing the rota. After putting so much effort into the business and getting it running so well, I didn't want to risk anything getting out of hand while I was away. You didn't say anything about how long you're likely to want me to stay.'

'Because I haven't the least idea,' I said. I had sat down opposite him. 'You'll have to talk to my friend, Anna Cox, about that. It was she who was so sure you could help her. She'd heard something about what you'd done in that Imogen Dale case and been very impressed, though I doubt if she got the whole story correctly.'

'I see. It was her idea that you should ask me to come down.'

I nodded.

He nodded too. 'It seemed too good to be true that you might have thought of it all by yourself. And actually it was just luck that you caught me because I was just going to go out to do a stint of work. D'you know, I believe I've found a job that really suits me.'

I had heard him say that so often as he changed from job to job that I was not very impressed.

'That work you had to do,' I said, 'do you mean to say you're actually going out cleaning other people's houses for them?'

'On occasion, in an emergency,' he answered. 'Most of the time I'm simply on the telephone, arranging other people's schedules, but there are times when someone's off sick, or had to go to his grandmother's funeral, you know the sort of thing, and then I may fill in, sooner than get the firm a bad name for being unreliable.'

'You go in that suit?'

'Of course not. I've got my working clothes, but you wouldn't have wanted me to come here in them, would you? Naturally I had to go back to the flat to change.'

'And you're head of this firm?'

'Not exactly. A partner. A man I'd got to know asked me to join him because he thought I'd got the right sort of personality for persuading people to use us. And I must say, I've found it extraordinarily interesting. One gets remarkable insight into the way all kinds of people live. You sometimes discover the most amazing things about them.'

'Things you could use?'

'What do you mean?'

I had not really meant anything, though for a moment I had a fearful vision of how Felix might be able to use his intimately acquired knowlege of his employers to blackmail them. But in fact I have never known him sink to blackmail.

'I was thinking how tempting it must be for you, when you see small precious objects that appeal to you, and nobody's watching you while you're busy cleaning and polishing,' I said, 'to slip them into your pocket.'

For an unfortunate thing about Felix is that he is not only a dedicated shoplifter, but except when he is in the house of a friend, where he in fact can be trusted, he is inclined to help himself to any odd things that catch his fancy. Before I had discovered that he did this and I had been deeply moved by his generosity to me, giving me all kinds of presents which I could not understand how he could afford, I had thought it a wonderfully endearing characteristic, and even after I had discovered that these things had not been paid for and that I was in fact a receiver of stolen property, I had thought of it as a psychological illness which perhaps a psychiatrist might cure. But he had stubbornly resisted the suggestion that he should visit a psychiatrist, for the truth was that he enjoyed stealing things and would have hated to be cured of the habit. He thought of it more as a kind of sport than as anything approaching a crime and he had never been able to understand why I should find it so unacceptable. I think he thought that as eccentric of me as I found what he did. Of course one of the reasons why I found his behaviour so particularly distressing was my certainty that sooner or later he would be caught, but so far this had never happened. Perhaps it would have been better for him if it had.

'You don't seem to understand,' he said with a certain air of sternness, 'that all of us who do this kind of work are in a position of trust. We are very careful about the people whom we employ, and so far there hasn't been a single complaint. And d'you know, if you can lay on a reliable cleaning service in some parts of London, it's a gold-mine. I expect it's quite different here in Allingford. You probably have some old dear who comes in and flicks her duster around and who's been coming to you for years and thinks of you as part of the family. But in some of the richer parts of London it's a very different story.'

It was not correct that any old dear had been cleaning my house for me. For some time the young, smart and efficient wife a local constable, who came to me mostly because she could bring her five-year-old daughter with her, had been doing that, but I understood what he meant. The personal contact was important, which in the great city it had no doubt ceased to be.

'Well, don't you want to know why I asked you to come down?' I said.

He dropped some cigarette ash into the ashtray that I had had the forethought to put out for him.

'Something about a murder,' he said, sounding a little bored. He would no doubt have preferred to go on talking about himself. 'A friend of yours?'

'Not exactly.'

'I'm glad of that. You aren't going to start crying on my shoulder?'

'Have I ever done that?'

'Unfortunately no, not that I can remember. But then you always were a cold-blooded fish. A tantrum now and then, but plain, honest tears don't seem to be your line. But there might always be a first time and really I shouldn't know how to deal with it. Who got himself killed, and what's it got to do with you?'

'It's a she, not a he,' I said, 'unless you count the dog. He was male.'

'A dog?' he said. 'You got me down here to investigate the killing of a dog?'

He sounded so shocked that I felt rather pleased. However, I said, 'The dog is only part of the incident. The main fact is that a young woman whom I knew only slightly was shot sometime yesterday evening when she was in bed, and a young man who is some kind of a cousin of hers has been taken in by the police for questioning. And between you and me, I'm inclined to think they've got the right man. He does seem to me to be the most logical suspect. But a certain old woman who really is a fairly close friend of mine is desperately upset at his being suspected, and made up her mind that you'd be the best person to clear him. So she asked me to get you to come down, and of course the first thing you must do is meet her.'

'And who is she, this old woman?'

'Her name's Anna Cox, and for the last thirty years or so she was housekeeper to a Mrs Lovelock, who was even older than Anna and who died a couple of weeks ago. And I got to know Anna because my mother used to play bridge with Mrs Lovelock who got into the way of asking me to visit her, even though I don't play bridge, and so I used to meet Anna and got to know her pretty well.'

'And what connection has she with this young woman who's been killed?'

'Oh dear, I'm afraid I'm telling this very badly,' I said. 'She's no connection actually. The young woman was a grand-niece of Mrs Lovelock's and was an actress who's been in Hollywood for the last two or three years, but who came over when she heard about Mrs Lovelock's death. And the young man the police have picked up is a grand-nephew of Mrs Lovelock's, who's lived in Australia since he was about thirteen, but came over to get to know his aunt a couple of months ago.'

'And is there anything suspicious about Mrs Lovelock's death?'

'Nothing whatever. She was eighty-eight and had a bad heart and the extraordinary thing is that she lived as long as she did.'

'You're sure of that?'

'Absolutely.'

'And the dog?' Felix said.

I realized that it had been a bad mistake to mention Boz, at least so early in the story that I was trying to tell. With his usual perversity, Felix was probably going to go on insisting that it was the murder of the dog that he had been called down to Allingford to investigate, and investigate it he would, however many young actresses from Hollywood might be lying cold in their graves or reduced to ashes in a crematorium.

'I think I'd better start from the beginning,' I said. 'We'll get to the dog presently.'

The best place to start, I thought, was Mrs Lovelock's funeral. I described how Anna had spoken to me after it, inviting me home for a sandwich and a glass of wine. I described how I had met Nick Duffield then for the first time, and Kate's late arrival. I also told him something about the other people who had been there and what I could remember of what we had talked about, and the presence of Boz. I told him that Mrs Lovelock had once bred Staffordshire bull terriers professionally and that I understood that at some time in the far past, when Nick had been a child, one of them had attacked him viciously and that Kate had remembered this and had mocked him with still being afraid of dogs, even Boz. I went on to describe how I had met Nick in the town the next day and how he had invited me to the bungalow to choose some memento of Mrs Lovelock.

When I reached that point it occurred to me how fortunate it had been that Felix hd not been there, because almost certainly he would have come away with more than one memento, quietly slipped into a pocket, and that he would not have been as careful as I had to take away something that was of no value.

'Now wait a moment,' he said when I reached that point, 'the people who were there yesterday afternoon, the people who, as I understand it, could conceivably have put poison into the dog's food, let me make sure I've got them clear. There was a woman with a dotty son . . .'

'Julia Bordman. Only her son wasn't with her yesterday. She took a paperweight away with her. She was there when I arrived.' I paused, then added, 'Anna Cox told me a very distressing story about Charlie. It seems that when Kate was a child and great friends with Charlie, who I suppose would have been ten years older than she was, he assaulted her sexually, and though Julia persuaded Mrs Lovelock to keep the thing quiet for Kate's sake as well as his, he was sent to a psychiatric hospital and was there for a long time. And even though he's at home now, Julia keeps an eye on him almost continuously. And it was obvious, when Kate suddenly came face to face with him when she arrived after the funeral, that she recognized him and remembered the whole event, though he certainly didn't recognize her. But it must have been because of that having happened that Julia went to the house yesterday without him.'

'And who else was there?'

'There was Mrs Lovelock's next-door neighbour, Paul Kimber. I think you know him. He told me he'd met you recently and that you told him you'd just got back from Singapore.'

Felix brushed Singapore aside with a wave of his hand. 'Yes, I know him slightly. A freelance journalist, isn't he? Writes mostly about gardening and birds and insects and so on.'

'Yes, and as a hobby he makes some rather charming jewellery. He sells it locally, though I don't suppose he makes much profit from it. He just does it for pleasure. But connected with that, something a little curious happened.' I told Felix about Paul's telephone call to me and his statement that Mrs Lovelock's highly prized emeralds were fakes. 'But the necklace seems to have been stolen,' I said, 'and by someone who knew the combination of the safe.

But that in itself doesn't seem to mean much, because a lot of people knew it. Mrs Lovelock was always getting people to open the safe for her. Anna said that her having a safe to keep her valuables in was really just a kind of pretence.'

'But wouldn't you say that the people to whom she told the combination were probably all fairly intimate with her?' Felix said. 'She wouldn't have told it to the chance burglar.'

'I suppose not, no.'

'And he wouldn't have known that the emeralds were fakes. Do you think anyone besides Kimber knew that they were?'

'The question is, were they?'

Felix looked interested. 'You think Kimber lied to you about that?'

'It crossed my mind.'

'To get the idea around that he at least couldn't have had any reason for stealing them?'

'Something like that.'

'But this call he made to you was quite some time before the murder of Kate Galvin that night?'

'Oh yes.'

'So he'd have had to have had it thought out well in advance, first the poisoning of the dog to stop it barking when he broke in in the night, then the call to you, then the murder and then the theft. But why the murder? Didn't you say Kate was in bed, with no sign of having been alarmed by someone breaking in?'

'So I understood.'

'Do you think there was anything between the two of them, Kate and Kimber?'

'Not that I know of, but I suppose it's possible.'

'Altogether the murder seems rather unnecessary. Who else was there?'

'There were the Hearns. Roderick and Margot. He's a

lecturer on economics at the Polytechnic here, and she's
recently written a rather successful detective story.'

'I've read it,' Felix said. 'It's excellent. She'll end up one
of the Queens of Crime.'

'They arrived some time after I did,' I said, 'and chose
a copy of *The Woman in White* that had Mrs Lovelock's name
written in it. A very tactful choice, I thought. And there
definitely was a connection between the two of them and
Kate.' I told him what Anna had told me of the probable
love-affair between Kate and Roderick, which had nearly
wrecked the possibility of his marriage to Margot ever
coming about.

'And even if Margot, say, had a motive for wanting Kate
dead when she saw signs of her husband's interest in her,'
Felix said, 'she would have had to come supplied with
poison for the dog, as well as knowing that Duffield would
be on his way to London and that Anna Cox was probably
heavily doped with sleeping-pills and unlikely to wake when
she heard a shot. Well, I suppose that isn't actually impossible. And was there no one else besides Kate herself and
Duffield?'

'I believe there was Dr Cairns,' I said.

'Who's he?'

'He was Mrs Lovelock's doctor for the last two or three
years. The old doctor she'd had for years retired and Dr
Cairns took over. Anna told me he came to the house after
I left and only stayed a few minutes because he said he was
very busy.'

'Now I find that rather interesting,' Felix said.

'Why?' I asked.

'Because he'd have known about Anna taking sleeping-
pills, wouldn't he? He probably prescribed them for her.
And he could easily have laid his hand on some poison for
the dog. A question is, however, would he have had time
to get to the dog's dish to put the poison into it? And these

other people you've told me about, could any of them have
done that?'

'All of them, I should think,' I answered, 'because the
front door was standing open when I arrived, so any of
them could have slipped in and gone to the kitchen before
ever appearing in the drawing-room.'

'But how could they have known in advance that the
door would be open?'

'I don't know. I dare say it didn't really happen like
that.'

'Do you know of any relationship between Cairns and
Kate?'

'No. But I don't know everything.'

'I think, as you said, I'll have to talk to your friend, Miss
Cox.' Felix lit another cigarette. 'Can you arrange that
fairly soon? And there was some mention of tea. I really
rather fancy a cup of tea now.'

I thought that the best way to arrange a meeting between
Felix and Anna was to ask Anna to come to my house. If
I took Felix to Mrs Lovelock's we might find that it was
still crawling with policemen and that it might be difficult
to explain what he was doing there. It probably would
not help matters that he had met Superintendent Dawnay
before, and although on that occasion Felix had actually
been very helpful to the detective, in fact perhaps because
of that very thing, he might not be very welcome. So I
telephoned Anna and she answered with eagerness that she
would come at once. She drove up to my house only about
twenty minutes later.

She was in the grey jersey dress that she had worn at the
funeral, with the inevitable raincoat over it. As I took this
from her and hung it up in the hall she suddenly put her
arms round me and kissed me. She smiled, but she looked
very tired.

'This is so good of you, Virginia—and of him too, to come,' she said. 'I've felt better ever since you told me he'd be coming. Somehow I can't talk rationally to that man Dawnay. It isn't that I've anything special against him. He's been quite kind to me really. But I get muddled and I lose my temper with him, and of course that doesn't help. But your husband will be quite detached. He isn't emotionally involved with anyone in the case. All he'll want is the truth.'

This seemed to me such an extraordinary statement to make about Felix that I did not try to answer it, but took Anna into the sitting-room and introduced her and Felix to each other.

As I did so, I had a very odd feeling that he instantly and unreasonably disapproved of her. I guessed that he had been expecting someone quite different, probably a gentle little old woman who would have looked well in a crocheted shawl and lace, and who would at once have displayed a desperate need to be supported by his masculinity. In fact, a dream out of a past century, though it is my belief that even in those days little old women were no more gentle and dependent than they are now, even if they wore caps and had mysterious pockets into which all kinds of things disappeared. And Anna really wanted very much to be able to depend on him, though this did not show. She looked squat and solid and independent.

Speaking gruffly as she shook his hand, she said, 'This is really so good of you, Mr Freer—or may I call you Felix? I've known your wife for such a long time, it seems only natural. I suppose she's told you everything that's happened.'

'I've heard her version of it,' Felix said as they both sat down. 'But I gather that most of it is simply what you've told her. So if I'm really to be of any help, and I'm very

honoured that you should think I might be, I think I ought
to hear it directly from you.'

The disapproval was not showing now and I thought
that perhaps I had been wrong about it and that he had
been merely surprised by her. And after all, she had never
had a great deal of charm. It was one of her misfortunes.
It usually took people a little time to begin to appreciate
her quality.

'Something's happened since I last spoke to Virginia
which I think perhaps she ought to hear,' she said. 'It's
about Boz—Mrs Lovelock's old dog.' She turned to me.
'It's been confirmed that he was poisoned, Virginia. His
supper was heavily laced with some kind of weedkiller.
They told me what it was, but I don't remember the name.
You know some of those things have some appallingly
poisonous chemical in them which can do birds and mice
and other small things quite a lot of harm if they get too
big a dose of it. But usually, of course, it's sprayed quite
thinly and it isn't dangerous, but when an old dog like Boz
gets a really strong helping of it in his food, he hasn't much
chance. So I'm afraid your idea that he might have got out
of the house and picked the poison up somewhere outside
won't stand up. It's a pity, isn't it? One wouldn't feel somehow so badly to blame if it had been some chance thing
over which one had no control. But I never really had much
hope of that. It would have been too much of a coincidence,
happening on the night when Kate was killed.'

'But do I understand that the fact that the poison was
definitely in the dog's food means that it was put there
by someone who must have been in the house sometime
yesterday?' Felix asked.

She nodded her big, heavy head.

'I'm afraid so.'

'Then I think I'd like you to tell me all you can about
those people,' he said. 'As you said, Virginia has told me

all she can about them, but I'd like to hear what you have to say.'

He was really doing it very well, speaking with just the cool detachment which was what she had told me she wanted from him and eyeing her with a kindly thoughtfulness. She drew a deep breath, then plunged into the story that she had told me. She gave brief descriptions of all the people who had been in the house the day before the murder, adding only that Boz's supper had not been put into his dish until about five o'clock, so that there was no need to think of anyone who could have got into the house earlier than that.

'And did anyone get in earlier?' Felix asked.

'No,' she said.

'You're sure of that?'

'Oh yes, quite. Why?'

'It's only that I was wondering if someone could have slipped in before you knew it and concealed himself somewhere. Virginia tells me that when she arrived at the house the front door was open, so that it's just possible that someone got in without your knowing. Was it a habit of yours to leave the door open much of the time?'

She looked worried. 'No, but . . . Well, that was Nick. He was very casual about it. He'd forget to lock the car and that sort of thing. He seemed to think we lived deep in the country. Perhaps it was a habit they had when he lived in the outback, and even the nearest neighbours were miles away, though he's lived in Sydney for long enough to have outgrown it. But he knew we were expecting several people that evening so he seemed to take it as a matter of course that we should leave the door open.'

'And whose idea was it that these particular people should be invited for this rather touching little ceremony of remembrance?' he asked, sounding dreadfully sympathetic and smooth, as if he indeed found it touching.

'I'm not sure.' Anna seemed confused. 'Perhaps it was Nick's. No, it was mine. Yes, I'm certain I thought of it first.' She seemed anxious not to let any blame for having had the idea that had had such disastrous consequences be attached to Nick. 'And of course it was I who chose whom to invite, except that it was Nick who invited Virginia, but naturally I'd have done that myself if he hadn't told me he already had.'

'I wonder if there's any way I could meet these people,' Felix said. 'Is there any way you could arrange it?'

She nodded energetically. 'Yes, of course you must meet them. And I know just how we'll do it. Virginia, if I may use your telephone, I'll simply ring them up and ask them to come here and I'll tell them why. I'll say we've invited—' She broke off, looking at Felix. 'Just what do you think I ought to call you? Can I say you're a private detective?'

'Why not?' he said. 'It isn't completely accurate, but I can't see any harm in it.'

'Very well, then. I'll say we've invited a private detective, or perhaps a private investigator who happens to be a friend of Virginia's would sound better, to come and help to clear Nick's name, and he wants to meet all the people who were present in Mrs Lovelock's house yesterday afternoon. Of course, they may refuse to come, and that in itself may be significant.'

'That friend-of-mine line isn't going to go over very well,' I said. 'Paul knows Felix already and he's liable to mention the fact that he's my husband. I'd stick to the truth, more or less. I'd say that my husband, who's had a bit of experience in private investigation, is here and is ready to offer his services to see if he can find out anything to prove Nick's innocence. And I hope I've got enough sherry and gin and whatnot to go round, as that'll help. Have you got all their numbers, Anna, or do you want the directory?'

'I've got them all here,' she said, patting her handbag,

then taking out of it a little address book and turning its pages. 'The Hearns—I'll begin with the Hearns. I should think Roderick's home from the Poly by now, if he's been there today, wouldn't you? Right, then, I'll go ahead.'

My telephone was in the hall and I left her to go to work at it.

In the end it was only Dr Cairns who declined to come. The Hearns, Paul Kimber and Julia Bordman all accepted the invitation.

Returning to the sitting-room, Anna said, 'You know, they all sounded rather glad to come. They sounded as sure as I am that Nick had nothing to do with the crime. But Julia's bringing Charlie. I'm not sure if that's a good idea, but I could hardly refuse to let him come. I don't suppose he'll quite understand what's going on, but you know how good and quiet he always is.'

'I'd rather like to know a little more about Charlie,' Felix said. 'I've been told that he once assaulted Kate sexually when she was a child and when I suppose he wasn't exactly grown-up himself, and that she never forgot it. But what actually happened, do you know?'

A flush of embarrassment coloured Anna's worn cheeks.

'Well, not *exactly*,' she said. 'I mean, she was terrified and came running in from the garden and burst into tears and said Charlie'd shown her something and wanted her to— oh, really I can't put it into words, Felix. I'm sorry, I just can't. But when Helen questioned her she just cried and said it was horrible and when Helen went to look for Charlie he started crying too and said he didn't know what was the matter with him.'

'You mean, he admitted it?' Felix said.

'That's how we took it.'

'But the only actual evidence against him is what Kate told you.'

She frowned uncertainly. 'Perhaps that's so. But of course

we knew what she meant. Not that he'd done her any actual *harm* yet, so far as we could make out, but when Helen brought him into the house Kate ran and hid and wouldn't come out till he'd been taken away.'

'And then he was sent to a mental institution?'

'I don't understand you!' Anna said, her voice rising. 'Are you suggesting it didn't happen?'

'I think he must have been reading up on his Freud,' I said. 'He's wondering if the whole thing was a fantasy of Kate's because she'd wanted it to happen and what really upset her was that it didn't.'

'That did occur to me as a possibility,' Felix admitted. 'And the tears and the terror . . . Well, she did turn into an actress, didn't she? Perhaps she'd some ability in that direction even when she was a child.'

Anna wrinkled up her nose with a look of disgust. 'I don't believe in all that sort of thing. I'm certain that whatever Charlie did, he frightened Kate badly. Anyway, what's that got to do with what happened to her last night? Charlie wasn't there. He couldn't possibly have put poison into poor Boz's supper.'

'I was only thinking that if there was any possibility that she'd accused Charlie falsely,' Felix said, 'and the result of it was that he was taken away from his mother, and she later found out that Kate had made up the whole thing, she might always have nursed a most bitter hatred of her. Perhaps that isn't too convincing really, but it could give Julia Bordman a sort of motive for murdering Kate. Revenge, I mean, a desire to pay her out that had festered over the years. And one's got to remember that Charlie may have inherited his mental peculiarities from someone.'

'You mean . . .' Anna caught her breath, then went on, 'You mean Julia herself may be mentally peculiar. May be insane. Actually insane. D'you know, I've never dreamt of such a thing, but it's really a very interesting idea.'

It was an idea that seemed to cheer her up remarkably.

'It doesn't seem to you simply impossible?' Felix said.

'I don't know,' Anna answered. 'It's entirely new to me. I'll have to think it over. But actually everything that's happened still seems to me simply impossible. The only thing I'm sure of, quite sure of, is that Nick isn't the murderer, even though he may have what seems a better motive than anyone else.'

'I've been thinking a good deal about Charlie,' Felix said. 'I've been told he's what people call mentally retarded, but just how stupid is he?'

'Stupid?' She pondered. 'I'm not sure that he's stupid at all. Just a bit—well, he's rather like a child who's never managed to grow up. But children can be very clever, can't they? I know he's very musical, and I think he reads a lot and is very happy watching television, though I don't know what books he likes, or which are his favourite programmes. But I know Julia has no problems, looking after him. She can always keep him occupied. And he's always very considerate and polite. In fact, if he were only about fourteen years old instead of in his thirties, you'd say what a nice, well-balanced boy he was. You'd never ask yourself if he was stupid.'

'What I was wondering is how reliable he would be at carrying out instructions he'd been given,' Felix explained. 'Would he remember them and do what he'd been told, or would he forget them and just get muddled?'

'I don't understand why you're asking that,' Anna said. 'Charlie wasn't there yesterday afternoon. He can't be involved in poisoning Boz.'

'Are you sure of that?'

I thought that I had begun to understand what Felix was thinking about and there was a certain interest in it, but it seemed to me to have a fatal flaw.

'You're thinking it's possible Julia brought Charlie with

her when she came to the house,' I said, 'and while she went in and started talking to Anna, keeping her occupied, Charlie slipped out to the kitchen and dropped the poison into Boz's bowl, then left again and waited for his mother in her car. And as things were, I suppose that just could have happened. But Julia can't have known beforehand that the door was going to be open. She can't have known there'd be any opportunity for Charlie to get in and leave again without being seen.'

Felix nodded. 'I know that's a difficulty. But I'm going to bear the idea in mind. We may find there was some way that Mrs Bordman herself could have seen that the door was left on the latch. Now, Miss Cox, can you suggest any reason why Paul Kimber might have wanted Kate dead?'

Anna was looking bewildered and was giving a shake of her head when there was a ring at the doorbell.

I assumed that it was the first of the guests whom we were expecting and went to the front door to open it, only a little surprised that any of the people whom Anna had telephoned could have arrived so soon. But it was not any of them who stood there. It was Detective-Superintendent Dawnay, with Sergeant Wells.

'Good evening, Mrs Freer,' the Superintendent said pleasantly. 'I'm sorry to trouble you, but I was told that Miss Cox was with you. When she left Mrs Lovelock's house she left a message with one of my men that this was where she'd be if she was wanted.'

'And you want her?' I said, suddenly uneasy. I wondered what could have happened that had made it an urgent matter for him to track her down. Also it worried me that he would inevitably meet Felix. Neither of them had particularly friendly feelings towards the other.

'She's here?' Dawnay asked.

'Oh yes. Come in.' I know that I did not sound welcoming, but I stood aside to let the two men enter.

His profession perhaps had made Dawnay more accustomed than most to being received without enthusiasm and his manner remained friendly.

'It's just that we have some information which I think Miss Cox will find interesting,' he said, 'and I should like to hear her comments on it.'

I took him and the sergeant into the sitting-room.

Anna sprang to her feet at once with a look of great anxiety on her face.

'Why have you come here?' she demanded. 'What do you want?'

Felix also got to his feet and he and Dawnay gave each other rather cold little nods, not actually hostile, but without any indication that they took any pleasure in meeting each other again.

'I thought you'd be interested to hear that we've found the gun and the emerald necklace,' Dawnay said to Anna. 'The fact is, we found them some time ago, almost as soon as we started searching. They were very casually concealed under a pile of old sacks in one of the dog-kennels at the bottom of Mrs Lovelock's garden. But there were certain things about them we wanted to check before asking you if there was anything you could tell us about them. Fingerprints first, of course. But there were none. And the emeralds. They look very fine, but it happens that there isn't a genuine one among them. At some time, and by the look of things it was probably long ago, all the genuine stones were removed and some very ingenious paste substituted for them.'

To my astonishment, after staring at him for a moment with her mouth a little open, Anna burst out laughing. It was shrill, hysterical laughter, very surprising to me coming from someone who had always seemed to me so stolid and strong-willed.

'Paste!' she cried, still tittering helplessly. 'Her precious emeralds were paste!'

'But it isn't the fact that they're paste that's most interesting to us at the moment,' Dawnay said. 'It's where we found them.'

CHAPTER 6

He explained. 'It makes fairly certain what I've been inclined to think from the first. The theft of the emeralds was only a blind. Anyone who'd come to the house simply to steal them wouldn't have left them there. They'd have been taken away.'

'That makes sense,' Felix observed.

'There's something perhaps I ought to tell you,' I said. 'I'd been told they were fake. I didn't know for sure whether or not they were, which is why I said nothing about it, but I suppose that was wrong of me.'

'Who told you they were?' Dawnay asked.

'Mr Kimber,' I said. 'He rang me up in the evening some time after I'd got home from Mrs Lovelock's house, after I'd chosen my memento of her, and he told me he was worried because the jewels weren't real and he knew the fact that they weren't was going to be discovered by the valuers who'd be coming in soon. He asked me what I thought he ought to do about it. The special reason he was worried was that some time before Mrs Lovelock had given him the necklace for him to repair the clasp. You know he makes a certain amount of jewellery. And he realized then that the stones weren't genuine and he'd got scared that he might be accused of the theft, even though he didn't actually do the job himself, but took the necklace to a firm in Bond Street, who'd corroborate, I understand, that the stones had already been substituted when he brought it to them.'

'But he didn't tell Mrs Lovelock about that?' Dawnay said.

'Apparently not,' I answered. 'I asked him why he hadn't and he said he hadn't wanted to upset her.'

'And what did you advise him to do?'

'I think I told him to tell Mr Duffield and Miss Galvin about it, and of course Miss Cox.'

'Which it seems he didn't do.'

'I don't know anything about that.'

'I haven't seen him all today,' Anna said. 'He did telephone earlier to ask what was going on, but hasn't had much chance to tell me anything.'

'But it seems, Mrs Freer, you had some doubts about his story,' Dawnay said to me. 'If you'd been quite certain he'd told you the truth you'd have said something about it to me, wouldn't you?'

'But when you questioned me this morning you said nothing whatever about the emeralds,' I said. 'I didn't know then they were missing. If you'd told me they were, I expect I'd have told you about Mr Kimber's call.'

All the same, I was not quite sure whether or not I should have done so. I remembered my own uneasy feeling that Paul, in that strangely unnecessary call he had made to me, might not have been telling me the truth, but might only have been preparing me to support him when the valuers came and identified the supposed emeralds as imitation. Then when I had heard from Anna, after Kate's death, that the necklace had apparently been stolen, I had felt that something that I had simply been told on the telephone was hardly evidence and that it was for Paul himself to tell the police what he knew. But now what he had told me had been corroborated by them.

'I suppose Mrs Lovelock didn't happen to know herself that the emeralds were false,' Felix said. 'Is there any possibility that she did, Miss Cox?'

The two detectives looked at her and after a moment, as she gazed at Felix in dismay, Dawnay said, 'That's an interesting suggestion. Do you think she could have done so, Miss Cox?'

She rubbed a hand across her lined forehead. 'I suppose it isn't impossible,' she said at length. 'What she told me about them was that her husband had given them to her and that they'd originally belonged to his grandmother. And now that I come to think of it, she did seem somehow amused about them. I thought it was at the idea of her ever wearing anything like that necklace. She always dressed so simply and wore hardly any jewellery. But even suppose she did know, what difference does it make?'

'Perhaps none at all,' Dawnay said. 'And it's certain the substitution couldn't have been done by Mr Kimber. Our experts say the work's typical of what would have been done as long ago as perhaps a hundred years. In its way, as an antique, the necklace may be quite valuable. And whether or not Mrs Lovelock knew the truth about it may not be of the least importance. However, it's probable that somebody did.'

'Who?' Anna demanded.

'If we knew that, Miss Cox, we'd probably know who did the murder,' he answered. 'Someone who knew how to open the safe took the necklace to make it look as if the theft was the motive for Miss Galvin's murder, but he made a few rather glaring mistakes. First of all, she was killed when she was lying quietly in bed and not because she'd got up and interrupted a thief. Then the necklace was carelessly and hurriedly hidden where it was almost certain to be found pretty quickly, which it wouldn't have been if the thief had come to the house simply to steal it. He'd have taken both it and the gun away with him. If he ever went away. You see, that's what we have to consider. The density of the fog last night may have upset someone's plans quite badly.'

'You're thinking about Nick Duffield!' Anna cried. 'But

you're wrong, you're absolutely wrong! Nick couldn't have done it.'

'Why are you so certain?' Dawnay asked.

'Because I know him.'

'You don't know how often that's been said by the nearest and dearest of people who've committed the most appalling crimes,' the detective said with a touch of sadness in his voice. 'But we aren't saying for the moment you're wrong.'

'All the same, you're still holding him, aren't you?' she said.

'But our investigations are continuing. For instance, we'll want another talk with Mr Kimber. Living next door as he does, he could easily have gone to the kennels, put the emeralds into one of them, then got home in a few minutes. The fog wouldn't have bothered him and if he'd done that, of course he'd have intended that they should be found, precisely to make us suspect Mr Duffield. And the same could be said of Mr and Mrs Hearn, living in Morebury Close as they do. But according to what Mrs Freer has told us, it was Mr Kimber who knew that they weren't worth all that much. What we know nothing about, however, are his relations with Miss Galvin. Could he have had any motive for killing her? Is there anything you can tell us about that, Miss Cox?'

She only shook her head and muttered, 'Nick didn't do it.'

I was thinking that if the detectives were to stay only a little longer they would meet Paul Kimber here and I did not want them to do that. I did not want them taking him perhaps to the police station for questioning before Felix had had a chance to do that. I was only half aware that I had this feeling, because I had not really begun yet to take seriously the part that Felix might be playing in the inquiry into Kate's death. But I knew that I wanted the superintendent and the sergeant to leave before my guests started arriving.

But they were not ready to leave yet. Dawnay still had a question to ask.

'I told you we found the gun and the emeralds together,' he said. 'The gun is a Luger, dating probably from the days of the First World War. Do you know, Miss Cox, if Mrs Lovelock had such a thing in the house?'

Her answer was prompt. 'Not to my knowledge, and I should think it most unlikely.'

'If she'd had it, you'd probably have known about it, would you?' he asked.

'I can't say that for certain,' she answered, 'but yes, I think that sometime or other she'd have mentioned it to me. I understand what you're thinking, of course. You're thinking that her husband was the right age to have been in the army in that war, and I believe he was, so he might have brought the gun home as a souvenir. And she might have shown it to Nick Duffield. She might even have given it to him as a gift, as he was her only male relative and she would very likely have thought that guns are usually the possessions of men. I just don't happen to think that occurred.'

'I see. Thank you.' He stood up. 'Still, we'd like to know where the gun came from. If Mr Duffield brought it with him from Australia for some reason, you'd think he'd have had difficulty getting it through Customs, though he might have managed it. But we aren't forgetting that among the other people who are likeliest to have been able to poison the dog there may be one whose father, or uncle, or grandfather even, may have been in the fourteen-eighteen war. Meanwhile, thank you for your help.'

It seemed to be meant to include the three of us, though I did not see what particular help we had given him. But at least he and the sergeant had decided to leave. They had been gone for about five minutes when our first visitors, the Hearns, arrived.

They had never met Felix before and when I introduced him they made a rather obvious effort not to show any curiosity as to why the husband from whom of course they had heard that I had been separated for a fair time should suddenly have appeared on the scene.

'I think it's such a good idea that we should have this meeting, Virginia,' Margot said. 'We realize that we and you and Paul and Julia must all be under suspicion as well as Nick, and a discussion may help to clear the air. Paul and Julia are comimg, I suppose.'

'Yes, and Charlie,' Anna said.

The recognition of my utter stupidity in not having grasped until that moment that I myself might be a suspect gave me a nasty shock. But Margot was perfectly right to include me in her list. I had been in Mrs Lovelock's house when poison could have been put into Boz's bowl. I knew my way about the house. I had actually entered the house through that very conveniently open door, and I had no alibi. I had no relative who had served in the First World War, but relatives were not the only source from whom guns could be obtained. Not that I should have known how to handle it if I had been able to get hold of one, but that would be a difficult thing to prove. It is said to be very difficult to prove a negative.

I saw a trace of amusement on Felix's face as he understood all too easily what was passing through my mind.

However, he said, 'I believe a certain Dr Cairns isn't coming.'

'Sherry?' I said to Margot. 'Gin? Whisky?'

'I'd really rather like whisky with just a very little water,' she replied. 'It's been a difficult day and I'd like something strong. The police came over to see us a little before lunch and told us what had happened. We'd guessed that some-

thing had, of course, because of all the police cars going by
and so on and we rang up to ask what it was. And they
questioned us for what felt like hours, though I suppose it
wasn't really so very long.'

'They searched our garden shed for what we'd got in the
way of weedkiller,' Roderick said, 'and I'm not sure if the
fact that we hadn't got any was in our favour or against us.
We used up the last of our normal supply a week or two
ago on our paths and patio and I threw the empty packet
on to a bonfire that I made last week. I told them that and
they wanted to know what kind it was and where I'd bought
it. As it happened, I'd had it for months, always meaning
to use it and forgetting about it and I couldn't remember
its name for certain. I believe they thought that peculiarly
suspicious. And naturally the only alibis we had were that
we'd been together and I don't believe the alibis husbands
and wives give one another are ever thought very impressive. All that we could insist on was that we had no motive
for harming poor Kate.'

'You'd *what?*' Anna said, her eyebrows lifting in a look
of extreme scepticism. 'Really, Roderick, don't take us for
fools. Everyone knows about you and Kate.'

At that moment the doorbell rang again.

It was Paul Kimber this time. He was wearing a dark
blue anorak over a sweater and jeans. Taking off the anorak
and dropping it on a chair in the hall, he followed me into
the sitting-room. On seeing Felix he looked quite pleased,
nodded casually to the Hearns and to Anna, then said that
it was beginning to rain.

'I wonder if everything would have been different if we'd
had rain yesterday evening instead of fog,' he went on. 'It's
no problem, driving through rain. What's brought you,
Felix? An idea that Virginia can do with a little protection?
She can't have been feeling specially easy in her mind, all

alone here, knowing that we've got a gun-toting muderer on the loose.'

It had been a shock to me only a short time before to realize that I could be considered as a suspect, but even then it had not occurred to me that I might be a second victim. That thought did not make much impression on me.

But I said, 'Felix can be very protective. Usually it's at a distance, but he has my well-being at heart. However, as you probably know, he's interested in murder and other morbid things. And Anna and I thought it would be a good idea for those of us who were at Mrs Lovelock's house yesterday afternoon and could have poisoned Boz to get together and have a talk without having any police present. You've only just missed Dawnay and Wells, incidentally. They've been here and they told us they've found the emeralds and the gun. They'd been rather carelessly dumped in one of the kennels in Mrs Lovelock's garden. Whisky, Paul, or gin, or sherry?'

'Yes, whisky, please, Virginia.' He sat down. 'You mean it, they've found the emeralds?'

'So they said.'

'And that's all they said about them? They hadn't found out—anything else about them?'

'Oh yes,' I said. 'They knew they were false. But it seems some expert of theirs had assured them that the faking was done years ago, so you've no need to worry that they're going to think you might have done it.'

As I brought him his drink I saw him relax.

'That's good news,' he said. 'I knew I was a fool to worry about it, but I couldn't help it. Not that I was thinking of murder when I telephoned you yesterday. I was only think- ing of what the valuers were going to find out.'

'But had you a grandfather or any other relative in the First World War?' Felix asked. 'Because that's where they think the gun originated. They've been asking Miss Cox if Mrs Lovelock had such a thing in the house. Her husband, you see, might have brought it home as a souvenir.'

Paul shook his head. 'My grandfather was a farmer and went on farming right through that war. And I've never owned a gun. Nasty things. If I'd ever inherited such a thing, I'd probably have got rid of it. Killing things has never much appealed to me.'

'What about weedkiller, Paul?' Roderick asked. 'Haven't the police been investigating your garden sheds?'

'Oh yes, but I don't use the stuff,' Paul said. 'It can kill birds, you know, and I like to induce all the birds I can to come into my garden. I put out grain for them and bits of stale bread and so on. Some of them seem to get to know me and come back again and again when I go out. Not that I think that man Dawnay believed me when I told him that, and I suppose he's quite right not to. If I'd really killed old Boz with the stuff, I should think the first thing I'd have done is remove every trace of it on my premises.'

'I should have thought some scientific person could check your statement,' Margot said. 'It wouldn't surprise me if they come and take samples of the gravel on your paths to find out if there's any poisonous substance there.'

'That's the detective-story writer talking,' Paul said. 'Some of you all but believe in magic. But they're welcome to come if they want to.'

Felix helped himself to sherry. 'Speaking as an outsider,' he said, 'I find it curiously interesting that you all seem rather more concerned about the death of the dog than about that of Miss Galvin. What it seems to indicate to me is that you're all convinced that it was one of you who were in the house in the afternoon who killed her, and not someone who only came in in the night. Because after all it could have been Miss Galvin herself who killed Boz.'

There was a moment of shocked silence, then Roderick said, 'Why ever should she do that?'

'Perhaps because she simply didn't like him,' Felix said. 'Or because she didn't want him barking and waking Miss Cox when she let someone into the house.'

'But she was in bed, asleep, when someone got in,' Anna protested.

'In bed, but how do you know she was asleep?' Felix asked. 'Sleeping isn't the only thing people do in bed, so I believe.'

Margot gave a hard little laugh. 'If you mean what I assume you mean, Mr Freer, I don't think Kate Galvin was a person who'd have worried much if a dog barking had announced that she'd a visitor.'

Just then the doorbell rang again and this time it was Julia Bordman with Charlie.

Julia came into the sitting-room with her long, bony, sharp-featured face looking angry. She gave Anna a glare, as if she were blaming her for something, gave a cold little nod to the Hearns, ignored Paul Kimber and then stared hard and curiously at Felix. A look of instant suspicion appeared in her singularly penetrating blue eyes. Charlie stood just behind her with the air that he often had of being slightly bewildered, but of hoping that he would be able to do whatever was expected of him.

She spoke to Felix even before I had had time to introduce him to her.

'You're Virginia's husband, aren't you? And you think you can help to clear up this mess we're in. Why should you be able to do that? What's wrong with leaving it to the police? I had them with me this afternoon and that superintendent seemed to me a very reasonable man. And I'm sure they've picked on the right person. It's obvious, isn't it?'

'It isn't, it isn't!' Anna cried. 'No one who knew Nick could think of him as a murderer.'

'You don't know what people can think when they're told wicked lies,' Julia said fiercely. 'I learnt that myself long ago. But that isn't the point. Someone who was there yesterday afternoon poisoned Boz and which of us except Nick Duffield had any motive for killing Kate? Had I? Had Paul? Had Roderick or Margot? Had Virginia? Or had you, Anna? Yes, had you, Anna?'

I thought that Anna was going to begin to cry, but she controlled it. If tears had come, they would have been tears of rage, not of grief.

'You know I hadn't, but hadn't you, Julia?' she said. 'You've always blamed Kate for what happened to Charlie. And Kate nearly ruined the chance Margot and Roderick had of getting married. And we don't know what relationship she had with Paul, but perhaps she knew something about Helen's emeralds that we haven't found out. And for all I know, even Virginia had something against her. But what I do know is that Nick would never have killed Kate to lay his hands on her share of Helen's money. He isn't greedy, he's wonderfully generous. He's promised to pay all my expenses at some really nice old people's home. And he never met Kate until after Helen's funeral.'

'Oh, but he had,' Julia said. 'He and Kate knew each other as children. And she mocked him because she believed he was afraid of old Boz.'

'And you'd call that a motive for murder?' Anna demanded. 'You're mad, Julia. I honestly believe you are. It's something we've been talking about. I don't know when it happened to you, but you really aren't sane now. You might be capable of anything.'

'So that's why you got me here, is it?' Julia said. 'To tell me that. Charlie, we're leaving.'

He was plucking at her sleeve.

'Mother, I don't understand,' he said. 'Kate Galvin's dead, isn't she?'

'Yes, she is,' she replied, turning towards the door. 'Come along.'

But he stayed where he was.

'And she was killed, like all those people on television?' he asked.

'Yes,' she answered.

'But I didn't do it, did I?' he said. 'I know I did something awful to her once though I never understood what it was, only that it was something awful. But I didn't kill her, Mother, did I? I might have liked to. I've often thought I'd like to be a soldier and kill people, but I really don't think I did this.'

It was Julia who started to cry. She dropped on to a sofa and dabbed furiously at her eyes with the backs of her hands. Charlie sat down beside her and put an arm round her.

'Don't,' he said. 'Please don't.'

Without asking her what she wanted, Felix poured out a stiff whisky and took it to her. She took it in a shaking hand and gulped it.

'You see what I have to put up with,' she said. 'You're quite right, Anna, sometimes I think I'm not really sane. I can manage all right most of the time, but sometimes it gets too much for me. Charlie's such a dear, he's so sweet and affectionate, I've never believed what that horrible child Kate said about him, and nor did his psychiatrist, it may interest you to know. If anyone needed a psychiatrist, it was Kate herself. Of course she made up the story of what Charlie did to her.'

As usual, she was talking about Charlie as if he were not there.

'I'm so sorry I said what I did, Julia,' Anna said. 'I know

I'm not myself. First Helen dying, then Kate, and then this thing about Boz, and now Nick being arrested—well, I know they haven't actually arrested him yet, but it's what they're going to do unless we can find some evidence to clear him. Don't you all want to do that? I swear he's innocent. Don't you want to see an innocent man set free?'

'A thing I don't understand, Anna,' Roderick said, 'is why the noise of the shot didn't wake you. Whether it was Duffield who did it or not, why didn't you hear it?'

'Because I'm a dope-addict,' she answered, her tone changing to bitter anger. 'I take a good dose of sleeping-pills every night of my life, with a drink of hot milk, and once I'm asleep the last trump wouldn't waken me. I've suffered from insomnia all my life, and Dr Raven, who you probably remember was here before Dr Cairns, put me on to them. I was very afraid of them at first because I felt there was something awful about being an addict, but Dr Raven assured me the pills would do me far less harm than my sleeplessness was doing me, and it turned out he was perfectly right. My health improved enormously once I knew I could sleep. And Dr Cairns has simply continued the prescription since Dr Raven retired. So that's why I didn't hear the shot.'

'It would be interesting to know,' Felix observed, 'who knew about your habit of taking those pills.'

Margot gave one of her giggling little laughs. 'All the things it would be interesting to know! Who knew Anna would be sure to be sound asleep when he wanted to commit murder? Who could have put poison in the dog's food? Who knew Nick would be on his way to London, because it's what he would have been if it hadn't been for the fog? Who knew the combination of the safe? Who knew the emeralds weren't genuine? Who hated Kate enough, or had enough to gain by her death, to have killed her? Answer any one of those questions and you've probably got the answer to all the others.'

'I'm not at all sure of that,' Paul said. 'I'm not sure the murder and the theft are connected.'

'But of course they are,' Margot said. 'Someone—and Anna believes it was one of us in this room—put poison into the dog's dish in the afternoon to make sure he wouldn't bark in the night. Then he came back after Nick had set off for London, broke into the kitchen, went into Kate's room and shot her. Then he opened the safe and took the emeralds, meaning, I suppose, to drive off somewhere with them and the gun and dump them in some pond or river, hoping the theft would be taken for the motive for the crime. But the fog made driving difficult, so he left the things in the only place he could find in a hurry. He would probably have been in a hurry because Nick in fact might already have come back to the house. That's how it all happened, unless, of course, in spite of what Anna believes, the obvious thing is true and it was Nick who'd been meaning all along to come back and shoot Kate, so that he could get his hands on her share of Mrs Lovelock's money. That's what I myself believe.'

'Well, I'm glad to hear you say that,' Paul said, 'because I was expecting you to say that the murderer was me. I think I'm the most promising suspect. I knew the emeralds weren't actually worth stealing and I live next door, so slipping down to the kennels to dispose of them temporarily, then getting back home, fog or not, would have been no problem. And knowing they'd be found almost immediately would have suited me, because that would have helped to incriminate Nick, who of course I had heard come into the house. The only thing I can't explain is why I wanted to kill Kate. Of course it's possible I once had an affair with her and I was taking revenge on her because she'd somehow treated me very badly. That's a possible motive, but you'd have some difficulty in proving it.'

'I don't think you're a more promising suspect than I am,' Margot said. 'I hated Kate—I'll admit it—I detested her. She did her best once to destroy my relationship with Roderick and when the two of them met after the funeral, I could see it in her eyes immediately that she was going to try again. That's a pretty good motive. Only I can't quite see myself doing anything so stupid as making off with the emeralds. Because it was stupid. The police saw through it right away.'

'If it's suspects we're looking for,' Roderick said, a look of what might have been amusement appearing in his big, intense, dark eyes, 'I don't think you ought to leave me out. Everyone knows Kate and I once had an affair, but they don't know why it came to an end. Isn't it possible that she found out something about me, for instance that I'd faked my degrees and would have lost my job on the spot if she'd exposed me? Or that I was already married, perhaps to her, so that my marriage to Margot was bigamous? Or that I'd once been fined for parking illegally? There are all sorts of possibilities once you start to consider them.' He looked round the room. 'Does anyone else want to compete? What about you, Virginia?'

'Oh, please, please!' Anna cried, wringing her hands. 'Won't you all please be serious? I asked you here to see if you could help me bring Nick home. I didn't mean anything against any of you. And I don't think you should make jokes about it. Just think of what he's going through now in a strange country, among strangers, with no one really worrying about him except me. And I'm just a stupid old woman who loves him, so no one wants to listen to me.'

Julia stood up. She had a look of frigid dignity. Charlie slipped his arm through hers, but for once she shook him off, which made him look pained and puzzled.

'The only person in this room who can seriously be suspected of Kate's murder,' she said, 'is myself. I'm the only person here who's glad that retribution came to her in the end and that she's dead. She did her best to ruin my life. I know she was only a child, but the child is mother of the woman. How was I to know that she wouldn't do something of the same sort again? I have no garden. I have never bought any weedkiller and I would never have killed that poor old dog. I'd as soon have been caught with the gun in my hand, killing Kate Galvin. Tell that to the police if you want to, Anna, and I won't withdraw a word of it. Now come, Charlie, we're leaving.'

She strode out of the room. Charlie followed her, but in the doorway remembered his good manners and turned and said good-evening to us all. Felix went quickly after them to see them out of the house. By the time that he returned to the room the Hearns were saying goodbye to Anna and to me. Paul lingered for another drink, saying that he hoped Roderick's facetiousness had not upset Anna and that what he himself had said had not done so either. She allowed him to think that it had and that if he had not begun the absurd business of everyone making out a case against himself we might have achieved something useful. I did not think that even if they had all tried to do this, anything would have resulted. Soon Paul finished his drink and went after the others. I asked Anna if she would stay to dinner.

'Thank you, it's very sweet of you,' she said, 'but I think it's time for me to go home too. Anyway, I couldn't eat anything. It gives one a strange feeling, I find, to think that one may have been in a room with a murderer. Now, Felix, that you've seen them all, what do you think of them? You've been very quiet.'

'I didn't think I'd anything useful to contribute to the conversation,' he said. 'I've just been listening.'

'And have you come to any conclusions?' she asked.

'Conclusions? You could hardly expect that yet.' Even if he had, I thought, he was most unlikely to tell her about them. He assumed an air of deep thoughtfulness, suitable to the part that he was playing. 'However, it was helpful to meet them.'

'And what will you do next?' she asked hopefully.

'Ah, you must give me a little time to think about that,' he said. 'Perhaps go home. Perhaps tell you I'm fairly sure that Nick Duffield is guilty. Perhaps have some idea that may be what you'll think useful.'

'No, you don't think Nick's guilty!' she cried. 'I know you don't! But of course I understand that you need time to think. So I'll be going home, Virginia, and thank you so much for all you've done. I'll have a little supper, then take my pills early and go to bed. I'm very tired. I don't believe I've ever felt so tired in my life. Good night, my dear. And good night, Felix. I'm sure you'll have thought of something by tomorrow.'

He saw her out to her car.

Coming back into the sitting-room, he said, 'What are we going to have for dinner?'

I was pouring out another drink for myself. I agreed with Anna that it gave one a strange feeling to think that one might have been in a room with a murderer.

'I'll think of something presently,' I said, sitting down on the sofa and putting my feet up. 'I feel extraordinarily tired myself, though all I seem to have done today is sit about and listen to other people talking. What did you really make of them all, Felix?'

'It seemed to me that every single one of them was capable of murder,' he answered indifferently, 'but I've no preference. But I'll tell you one thing I think. I think you're all making much too much of that fog. People do drive through fog, you know, in fact a lot of them take almost no notice of it and drive a hell of a lot too fast, and if I'd just committed a murder and stolen some emeralds which I thought were valuable, I shouldn't have stayed around, dumping the emeralds and the gun in the garden and pretending I'd been frightened of driving. I'd have made off as fast as I could, fog or no fog.'

'So you don't think Nick Duffield's guilty,' I said, 'simply because he did stay around.'

'Look, have we got to go on talking about this?' he asked. 'If you're tired I'll get us something to eat, if you'll tell me what you've got in the place.'

'But don't you want to talk about it?' I said. 'Isn't that why you came? You're going to be a great detective and find out the truth.'

'I'll tell you why I came,' he said. 'It's because for the first time that I can remember you actually invited me to come. Do you realize you've never done that before? I've been here from time to time, either because I was passing through and thought I'd drop in, or because we'd business of some sort to see to, and I can't say you've ever actually slammed the door in my face, but I'm sure I've never before been invited to come. So now tell me what I can cook and I hope it's something decent, because I'm hungry.'

'There are two steaks in the fridge,' I said. 'I meant them for our lunch today, but you didn't turn up.'

'Steaks,' he said. 'Steaks, salad, ice-cream, coffee, is that the menu?'

'If you want it,' I said. 'I've got the steaks and there are all the things you need for a salad, and I've some ice-cream in the freezer, and of course I've got coffee.'

'Steaks, salad, ice-cream, coffee,' he murmured musingly, as if it were a kind of chant. 'You know, it's an extraordinary thing but when I was in America recently that was exactly what everyone gave me to eat. One nice hospitable person after another gave me just that.'

'You've never been in America,' I said, 'so how could they do that?'

'Now why do you say a thing like that?' he asked. 'Of course I've been there.'

'Exactly when?'

'Oh, since I saw you last. I forget when that was. But I was in New York for about a fortnight.'

'I don't believe it,' I said. 'You're too dead scared of aeroplanes to have flown even across the Atlantic, and ships make you seasick.'

'I admit I was scared, flying. I've never tried to pretend otherwise. It's claustrophobia. But one can control that if it seems important enough. One can even outgrow it.'

'Why was it so important to go there?'

'Because everyone one knows has been there sometime or other. It feels stupid to have to say one's never seen New York. And I got to know a nice chap from Columbia University, over here on a grant, and he urged me to go over with him and he introduced me to a lot of people and they were wonderfully hospitable. I was always being asked out. And everywhere I went they gave me a steak, salad, ice-cream and coffee. All of it excellent. I've never had such good steaks. But it had a curious effect on me. By the time I got home there was only one thing I wanted and that was a shepherd's pie. It became an obsession. I kept thinking about it, a shepherd's pie with a lovely thick brown crust of mashed potatoes on top and nice mince and a lot of onions and gravy inside. I once had a dream about it.'

'Shepherd's pie in the sky by and by,' I said. 'Felix, try to remember, this is Virginia you're talking to. I don't believe a word of it.'

He frowned. 'Why not?'

'Because I still don't believe you've been to America. I've heard you tell people, and almost convincing them, how you once crossed the Greenland ice-cap on skis, and about

how you got lost in the Australian desert and were rescued
by a tribe of aborigines who stole your clothes and fed you
on maggots, but saved your life. And all the time you'd
really been staying daydreaming in your flat in Little Carbery Street after listening to someone talking in a pub about
what he'd done, which for all you knew, could have been
as much of a yarn as anything you've told me. And that's
what I think has happened now. You've chatted to someone
who told you about his experiences in New York and you
thought it made a nice story. Well, I'm sorry I can't lay on
shepherd's pie for you tonight, but I'll see what I can do
tomorrow.'

He gave up trying to convince me. 'So tonight it's steak,
salad, ice-cream and coffee.'

'I'm afraid so.'

'I don't really mind.'

'I should hope not.'

'But I wonder why you really asked me down here,' he
remarked as he went to the door. 'Somehow I can't believe
it was just about a thing like murder.'

CHAPTER 7

Next morning I went to the supermarket and bought a frozen shepherd's pie. I had had one once before and it had not been at all bad. I also bought a tin of creamed rice and one of fruit salad. If I had had longer notice that I should be having Felix as a guest I should probably have laid in supplies of more interesting things, but in any case, I thought, it was unlikely that I should have felt in a mood for cooking that day. Murder does not whet the appetite.

By next day perhaps, if he was staying, I might do better. Then I remembered that next day I had some appointments at the clinic and would not have much time for cooking. But with luck he might offer to take that over himself as he is a far better cook than I am and cares a good deal more than I do about what he has to eat. While I was out I went into the bank and cashed a cheque, as having Felix to stay could turn out expensive. He was liable to suggest that he should take me out to dinner at the Rose and Crown and I should find myself paying for it, though he would of course promise to repay me next day when he had been to the bank himself. Somehow he always managed to have left his credit card at home. Not that I was sure that he actually had one. The temptation it offered to accumlate debt might have scared him. He was scared of all sorts of things besides ships and aeroplanes, though unfortunately never of being caught shoplifting or telling his colourful stories about himself.

I found him when I returned home in what was for him unusual company, for he does not usually care for entertaining the police. But Superintendent Dawnay and Sergeant Wells were in the sitting-room with him drinking coffee. All three of them were smoking and the atmosphere, though nauseous to breathe, appeared to be amiable, if serious. The faces of all three men were grave. They got to their feet as I came in and Dawnay said, 'I'm glad we've managed to see you after all, Mrs Freer. I was afraid we should miss you. We've some other visits to make. Something happened last night—we've just told Mr Freer about it—but we'd like to know if you can add anything to what he's told us. Miss Cox was here yesterday evening, wasn't she?'

'You know she was,' I said. 'You met her.'

'And I believe she stayed for some time after we left,' he went on.

'Yes,' I said as I sat down.

They all sat down too. The superintendent's pale eyes had their usual look of curiously expressionless acuteness. He did not want to miss anything that I might show, but did not want to betray himself noticing it.

'Can you tell me roughly when she left?' he asked.

'I should think it was about half past seven, or perhaps a quarter to eight,' I answered. 'I asked her to stay for dinner, but she wanted to go home.'

'Mr Freer has told us she said that she was going to take her sleeping-pills with hot milk and go to bed.'

'I believe she did.' I suddenly began to feel anxious. 'Why, has something happened to her?'

'She appears to have taken a large overdose of the pills,' he said. 'She was found in her bed this morning, by the woman who goes in daily to clean.'

'Dead?' I exclaimed.

'Not quite, but not far off it. She'll recover.'

'She will? You're sure?' The words almost stuck in my throat. 'Is she in hospital?'

'No, Dr Cairns advised us to leave her where she was to sleep it off.'

'She's still unconscious, then?'

'She was when we left. A nurse is with her, one who sometimes attended on Mrs Lovelock, and a WPC. I've just put a call through to the house and the girl says she seems to be in a state of normal sleep now. But there's no chance yet of questioning her.'

'So you came to question me. But I can't tell you why she did it. I know she's been under a great strain recently, and she's been particularly upset by your suspicions of Nicholas Duffield, partly because of what he'd promised to do for her, I suppose, but also because she really seems to care for him. But it never occurred to me when she left here yesterday that she was anything like suicidal.'

'We aren't entirely certain it was attempted suicide,' he said. 'It could have been attempted murder.'

I could not think of anything to say, I only stared at him, meeting the gaze of those strange eyes of his, and for a moment they held me as if I were hypnotized. Then I managed to turn my head and spoke to Felix.

'You've heard this already?' I said.

'Yes, we've been talking it over,' he replied, but with a certain remoteness as if he did not want to be drawn more into the discussion than he could help.

I looked back at Dawnay. 'What makes you think of murder?'

'I wouldn't say we do think it,' he answered. 'I only mentioned it as a possibility. We shan't really be able to tell much until we can talk to her, if then.'

'What do you mean by "if then"?'

'Merely that she may not want to tell us the truth. Suicides often don't.'

'But you said just now you aren't sure it was suicide.'

'I'm not barring the possibility. It could have been, though there are certain things it's hard to explain.'

'Are you going to tell me what they were?'

He seemed to hesitate for a moment, then he said, 'Well,

to begin with, there are traces of the drug that she took in a nearly empty milk bottle in her refrigerator. There are also some in a small saucepan that she'd left in the sink and in which she'd apparently heated up the milk she'd drunk sometime that evening. That in itself isn't so strange. She may have thought that the easiest way to swallow a considerable number of her pills was if they'd been dissolved in the hot milk. But in that case, why the traces in the milk bottle? Why put them in the milk bottle first and then in the saucepan? But if someone else had left them there for her to swallow, the bottle would have been the obvious place to put it. And that brings me to a question I'd like to ask you. I've already asked your husband and I'd like to know if you can add anything to what he's told me.'

In other words, he wanted me to confirm what Felix had told him. His policeman's instinct had told him that it might not be wise always to accept without corroboration what Felix had to say.

'Yes?' I said.

'How many people do you know of who knew that Miss Cox always took sleeping-pills with a mug of hot milk before retiring?'

I gave a shrug of my shoulders. 'Possibly lots of people. I can't possibly guess.'

'How long have you known it yourself?'

'I think since yesterday morning, when you mentioned it to me.'

He nodded. 'Yes, I remember. It explained why she hadn't heard the shot that killed Miss Galvin. But I understand from Mr Freer that she spoke of it yesterday evening, when several people were here.'

'That's right, she did.'

'So that all those people knew about it.'

'Yes, but there may have been others too.'

'Of course. But Mr and Mrs Hearn and Mr Kimber and Mrs Bordman definitely heard her say that she took sleeping-pills every evening with hot milk?'

'Yes, and Charlie.'

'Charlie?'

'Mrs Bordman's son.'

'Oh yes, the one who's not quite with it. Perhaps we needn't trouble ourselves about him.'

'And what are your other reasons for thinking it could have been attempted murder? You spoke just now as if there were more than one.'

He nodded again. 'It appears that the bungalow was searched at some time during the night. The safe in the drawing-room was open and papers from it were scattered on the floor. Drawers and cupboards in the other rooms were apparently ransacked. It looks as if it was a hurried job, messy and unmethodical, as is common enough in some burglaries. But I'd be surprised if this was an ordinary burglary. Apart from the emeralds which were removed the night before, there were several oddments of jewellery in the safe, not highly valuable, but certainly worth taking if theft was the object. And money in Miss Cox's handbag had been left. Papers of some sort strike me as more probably what was wanted. Someone who knew how to open the safe went to it first, failed to find what he was looking for in it and went on searching, even in Miss Cox's room. She would of course have been unconscious by then.'

'And how did whoever did this get into the house?' I asked. 'Oh, of course, from the kitchen. The window there was broken the night before, wasn't it?'

'Yes, but it had been repaired and hadn't been broken again. And the lock of the front door hadn't been forced. Our intruder got in quite easily with a key. And that brings me to something else I wanted to ask you. Who do you know of apart from Miss Cox, Miss Galvin and Mr Duffield, who might have had a key to the house?'

'I believe Mr Kimber had one,' I said. The thought depressed me, because I rather liked Paul and did not want to tell tales against him. 'Miss Cox insisted that he should have one in case she locked herself out of the house one day and Mrs Lovelock for some reason didn't hear her ringing or knocking. I don't believe Miss Cox ever did lock herself out, but she told me once she felt safer if she knew someone else had a key.'

'And that's all you know?'

For some reason I had a feeling that he himself knew something that I did not, but I answered, 'Yes.'

'And Mr Kimber left here yesterday evening some time before Miss Cox?'

'A little while, yes.'

'Long enough for him to have gone to Mrs Lovelock's bungalow, let himself in quickly with his key and put the dope in Miss Cox's bottle of milk?'

'I doubt it, but I suppose it's just possible.'

'But the one person who couldn't have done that, even if he had a key,' Felix said, 'is Nicholas Duffield, who happens to be in your hands.'

'I'm aware of that,' the superintendent said coldly. 'But I'd still like to know, Mrs Freer, if you've ever heard of anyone besides Mr Kimber having a key to the house, or ever having had one in their hands; it needn't have been recently. A copy of a key can be made quite quickly.'

'That means you're thinking these crimes could have been planned some time ago,' I said.

'Only if the person who committed them knew that Miss Galvin was likely to come here at some time. She could have been planning to do so quite apart from coming to her aunt's funeral and someone with whom she'd perhaps been in correspondence may have known that.'

'You're making it sound awfully complicated,' I said, 'but I'm afraid I can't help you. I don't know of anyone but Mr Kimber who ever had their hands on a key of Mrs Lovelock's house. That doesn't mean that no one else did, but I don't know about it.'

'Didn't Miss Cox once lend you a key, Mrs Freer? Mrs Lovelock's daily help, Mrs Redman, says she did.'

I realized then that it had been to ask me that question that the detective had come to the house. And of course he was perfectly right, I had once had the key to the bungalow in my possession, though it was so long ago that I had forgotten about it. All the same, I felt a most unpleasant sensation, a kind of chill, along my spine.

'Yes, I remember,' I said, 'but it must be, oh, at least two years ago. Miss Cox was going to London to do some shopping for Mrs Lovelock and wanted to stay there for the night to go to a theatre. She didn't have much chance to do that sort of thing usually. And she wanted me to spend the day with Mrs Lovelock, because she didn't like leaving her all alone, so she left me her key so that I could come and go. And I remember gossiping with Mrs Redman. I suppose that's what she's remembered. And I did the cooking and played a double-demon with the old lady and fed Boz. Poor Boz. If only I'd taken him away with me that evening when I first suggested it he wouldn't have been poisoned. Yes, I'm sorry, Mr Dawnay, I didn't mean to mislead you, but I did have the key for a day. But I didn't burgle the house last night.'

Felix broke in rather sharply, as if he resented the question that I had been asked. 'Whoever shot Kate Galvin could have helped himself to her key, knowing that he'd be ruturning later, couldn't he? Had she a key in her handbag or anywhere else?'

'Actually, no,' Dawnay said. 'And it's possible she never had one. She'd arrived only a short time before. She may not have been given one yet. That's something Miss Cox may be able to tell us when we're able to question her. But it's possible also, as you say, that her murderer took her key so that he could come back. He may have intended to search the house after he'd killed her, but if he heard Mr Duffield return he'd have left as quickly as he could. He and Mr Duffield may actually have been in the house at the same time, though it's more likely, I should think, that he heard the car being driven into the garage and that warned him off.'

'Miss Cox will be pleased Mr Duffield couldn't have doped her drink or searched the house,' Felix observed. 'And in that case I may be going home. Perhaps we shan't meet again.'

Dawnay did not answer, but got to his feet and for a moment stood still, looking thoughtful, then, as if it were a new idea, suddenly thanked us as usual for our help, said goodbye and left, followed by the sergeant.

Felix saw them out of the house and as he returned to the room I said, 'Are you really thinking of going home already? I got such a nice shepherd's pie for lunch.'

He went back to the chair where he had been sitting and lit a cigarette. He was frowning and as he did not seem inclined to reply I started for the kitchen to put the shepherd's pie in the oven and to cook a cauliflower that I had. I also had the tins of creamed rice and fruit salad to open. But before I reached the door Felix remarked, 'That man doesn't think it was suicide. Nor do I.'

'I don't think I do either,' I said. 'I can't think of any reason why Anna should want to kill herself.'

'And you're sure Kimber has a key to the house?'

'Oh yes. But are you going or staying?'

'I don't think I'd much like to be in Kimber's shoes at present.'

'Felix, you haven't answered my question. Are you going home?'

'Do you want me to go?'

'It's entirely for you to decide.'

'I see. Well, let's talk about it after lunch. What about a drink now?'

'All right. I thought you might want to go because Nick's been cleared of doping Anna, and it was only to clear him that she wanted you to come down. But I've just thought of something. It's something I don't think I told you about yesterday. You know how Dawnay seems to think it was papers the burglar last night was looking for and about the safe being open, with papers from it scattered on the floor?'

'Yes.'

'Well, there's a little thing that happened when we were all choosing our mementoes of Mrs Lovelock. The safe was open and Nick suddenly brought out what looked like a little packet of letters and threw them into the fire. He said they were letters he'd written to his aunt from Sydney, and that it was what he'd always done with old letters. He said he hated the thought of them getting into the wrong person's hands and having them pawing through his secrets, however harmless they were. And Kate said she thought Nick had more secrets than one might suppose and that they weren't necessarily harmless.'

Felix looked interested. 'And did Kate sound serious, or simply facetious?'

'I don't know. Nick said to me that she'd taken a dislike to him. Perhaps she was just trying to get under his skin in some way.'

'You wouldn't think he'd have written anything desperately indiscreet to his grand-aunt.'

'No.'

'Who else was in the room at the time?'

I had to think for a moment. 'Julia Bordman was there,

and I think Paul had come in—yes, I'm sure he had.'

'But not the Hearns?'

'No, they came a little later.'

'So if by any chance it was that bundle of letters someone was looking for last night, it wouldn't have been Julia or Paul, as they'd both have known it had been destroyed.'

'Yes, but it could have been somebody else. It probably was. I only mentioned it because it was an odd little incident. Now what about that drink you thought you'd like?'

He seemed to have forgotten about it, then said yes, of course, if it was what I wanted, as if he had not been the first to suggest it. I left him to start operations in the kitchen and when presently I returned, wanting my sherry, I found him lying on the sofa, a cigarette in his hand but with his eyes closed. As I poured out sherry for us both I reminded him that he still had not told me if he was going or staying.

'Oh, staying, if you don't mind,' he said. 'Even if they let Duffield go because he couldn't have been involved in last night's troubles, he hasn't actually been cleared of Kate's murder, has he? It's possible, you see, that what happened last night was a result of that murder having happened. Perhaps there'd have been no need for it if Kate hadn't been dead.'

That afternoon I had to spend a couple of hours at the clinic. It was as I emerged from it at about four o'clock that I met Margot Hearn. She was coming out of the library with several books in a basket, and she was about to get into her car when she saw me. She hesitated for a moment, then came towards me.

'What about coming home with me for a cup of tea?' she said.

Her pale, oval face was more heavily made-up than usual and the brown hair that usually fell loose on her shoulders had been smoothed back and tied with a scarlet ribbon.

She was wearing a scarlet suit with a black, high-necked jersey and dangling gold earrings. She was generally very careless about how she dressed, so I wondered why she was so elegant today. Was it the way murder and police inquiries affected her? Did dressing up a bit improve her morale? But she explained it.

'I've just been to lunch and then had to speak at the Allingford Women's Book League,' she said. 'It was stupid of me to agree to do it. Speaking isn't one of my things, though I've done it a few times since my book was televised. Of course I simply read a paper I'd written, but then I had to answer questions, and it seems there's only one thing people want to know about writers and that is if you write by hand or straight on to a typewriter? It's always been the first question I'm asked. But oh God, Virginia, I'm so tired of questions at the moment. I had that man Dawnay with me this morning, asking questions about the pills I take. Well, can you come home with me for that cup of tea?'

I thanked her, but said that as I had my own car parked outside the clinic I had better follow her in it out to her house. She changed her mind then and suggested that we should have our tea in the small café on the other side of the street. We went in and soon found ourselves sitting at a small table. I said that I did not want anything to eat, but she ordered a toasted crumpet.

'Actually I'm ravenous,' she said. 'The lunch they gave me was miserable. Why don't women treat themselves better when they do that kind of thing? I can't see a lot of men being satisfied with what we had, a fishy sort of thing and not even any wine. But in any case I couldn't have eaten anything, I was too nervous. Not just because of the speaking, but because of the police turning up just when I was getting ready to go out. I told them I'd got to go and luckily they didn't stay long, but it upset me.'

'And they asked you about pills?' I said.

'Yes.'

'Do you take a lot?'

'Not a lot. Just a couple now and then.'

'Sleeping-pills?'

'Yes, of course that's what they wanted to know about. You know about what happened to Anna last night, don't you?'

'Yes, I had the police round this morning and they told me, but they didn't ask me any questions about pills.'

'Perhaps you don't take any.'

'Just the odd paracetamol now and then.'

'Well, you see, they'd seen Dr Cairns before they came to me and he told them he sometimes prescribes sleeping-pills for me, as he did for Anna. He gives me the same kind as hers. So they'd got it into their heads I could have slipped some into her milk bottle before Roderick and I came round to your house. We knew she was there, because that's where she'd telephoned from, so we knew Mrs Lovelock's house would be empty. And living as near to her as we do, it would have taken us only a few minutes to do it. Roderick would have had to be in on it too, but he wasn't at home this morning when they came round, so I had to cope with them by myself. Only they didn't explain how we got into the house without a key as we'd have had to have managed somehow, because it seems that the kitchen window, which was broken the other night, had been repaired immediately and it hadn't been smashed again. But they didn't seem much interested in that. Yet whoever got in yesterday evening must have had a key and simply gone in by the front door.'

The words were pouring out of her faster and faster. I had never known her so nervously loquacious.

'They asked me about the key,' I said, 'and I admitted I'd had one in my possession for a day a couple of years ago when Anna went up to London and wanted me to keep an eye on Mrs Lovelock. But I don't think they believed I'd been plotting to kill Anna for two years.'

'I don't believe anybody's been plotting to kill Anna,' she said in the same swift, jerky fashion. 'I think it's obvious she took the stuff herself.'

'Felix doesn't think so,' I said. 'He said he doesn't believe it was suicide and that Dawnay doesn't either.'

'That husband of yours,' she said, 'he really knows a lot about that sort of thing, does he? Is there any reason why he should know any more than the rest of us? Doesn't he know that people sometimes take poison simply to draw attention to themselves, but haven't any intention of dying?'

I only knew that Felix had an odd way of being right when it came to interpreting the behaviour of other people. In his way he was very intuitive. If he had been as good at interpreting what was at the bottom of some of his own behaviour, he might have had an outstanding intellect.

Margot went on, 'But it could have been an accident, you know. Anna's been in a very wrought-up state these last few days and she could easily have forgotten she'd put one dose of pills into her milk already and simply added another one. People do do that sort of thing.'

'You think that's how she actually took her pills, do you?' I asked. 'I mean that she dissolved them in the milk and then drank it down? I somehow thought of her simply swallowing them first and then drinking the milk afterwards.'

'Do you know that that's what she did?'

'No, I don't know anything about it.'

'I wonder if Cairns knew about the milk.'

I was puzzled and looked at her with curiosity. 'Does it make any difference if he did?'

'Only that he can lay his hand on more pills than any of us,' she said. She spoke more calmly now, almost with amusement. 'I'm not really serious, I don't suspect him. But it's true, isn't it? He's got loads of pills in his surgery and might even have had some poison that could be used on old Boz. And after all, he was in the house for a short time the evening Kate was shot. And he could have poisoned Anna simply by putting some pills of double or treble strength in among the ones he normally prescribed for her. He needn't have had to get hold of a key to get into the house at all. I know if he did that he couldn't have known when she'd take them and it would have been sheer chance that it happened the night we'd all been in your house, discussing Kate's murder.'

'But why should he have wanted to kill Anna?' I asked. 'What was his motive?'

'It would have to be that she knew something about him that would have ruined him if she'd let it out.' She gazed at me steadily for a moment, then burst out laughing. 'Your face, my dear! You're forgetting my new profession. I believe I could spin a yarn about even you if I gave my mind to it. In fact, you'd be a pretty good suspect, being about the most unlikely person to have murdered Kate. You see, that's how my mind works nowadays. Who, I have to ask myself, who was in the house the evening Kate was murdered, had absolutely nothing against her? I think it's you.'

As the one person who certainly knew that was true, I smiled as I shook my head.

'You'll have to do better than that. Who's the next most unlikely?'

'Charlie.'

'But Charlie wasn't there.'

'He was, you know. He was sitting in Julia's car when Roderick and I arrived. We even spoke to him. He was sitting in the passenger's seat with his seat-belt done up so that he looked as if he'd been strapped in. Perhaps he really was. Perhaps he didn't know how to undo it. Anyhow, he asked us if we thought his mother would be long, because he didn't like sitting there alone in the dark.'

I remembered that I had wondered myself if Julia might have brought Charlie with her that evening and left him outside in the car.

'I think the whole thing would have been a bit beyond Charlie's mental capacity,' I said.

'Which is what makes him so unlikely and therefore so probable. However, if you'd prefer to discuss the likeliest person, whom do you fancy?'

'Paul has a key to the house . . .' As I said it, however, I suddenly had a sense that what she was doing, talking to me as she was, was probing to see if I would show any suspicion of her. Yet she must have known that even if I had had such a suspicion, I would not put it into words, sitting there in the little café, drinking our tea. But with her singularly observant dark eyes on my face, I felt that I was being watched for something that might betray what my feelings were.

I doubt if she saw anything that gave her any reason for reassurance or for fear.

'Paul,' she said thoughtfully. 'Yes, Paul. It almost has to be Paul, doesn't it?'

'Except that, according to your view of things, the likeliest person ends up being the most unlikely.'

She laughed again. 'Which makes him the most unlikely, had you thought of that? But how right are you. However, we'll forget Paul.'

'Only I don't think Superintendent Dawnay is going to forget him,' I said. I finished my tea. 'Margot, you know the story about Charlie and Kate, don't you? I mean, what happened when Kate was a child and Charlie still hardly grown up?'

'I've heard it from Julia.' Her tone was suddenly serious.

'What do you think about it? What really happened?'

'I don't suppose anyone will ever know,' she said. 'Charlie's psychiatrist may think that he does, but even he could be wrong. And Charlie himself is the last person who could tell you anything.' She finished her tea too. 'So you're thinking about Julia.'

'It's only that she'd a real hatred of Kate.'

'But so had I. I've made that clear, haven't I?'

Almost too clear, I felt like saying, but in fact did not answer her. We both stood up, paid for our tea, parted outside the café and went to our cars.

I had an urge to report the whole conversation to Felix while it was fresh in my mind, I was not sure why, because I did not think that anything very illuminating had been said, but when I reached Ellsworthy Street I found that Felix was not at home. The house was empty.

He came in about an hour later and when I asked him where he had been he told me that he had been to see Dr Cairns. He had found the address in the telephone directory, but had not been able to see him until Dr Cairns arrived for his evening surgery. Even then Felix had had to wait for some time and it was his impression that the doctor had not wanted to see him.

'There were several patients queueing up for their interviews,' Felix said. 'His secretary didn't want to let me in. But I promised it wouldn't take long and said that it would be simpler than if I had to chase him to his home.'

'What did you want to see him about?' I asked. 'Anna's pills?'

'Among other things. As a matter of fact, he wouldn't tell me anything about pills. Said that sort of thing was confidential and it wasn't as if I was police. And he wouldn't tell me how near Anna got to doing herself in.'

'I thought you were fairly sure it wasn't she who'd tried to do herself in.'

'I didn't actually say that, did I? It's true I'd have been

surprised if she had. But even if someone else doped her milk, she did take it herself, didn't she? Though that's a bit beside the point.'

'I met Margot this afternoon,' I said, 'and she told me she takes the same pills as Anna and that she'd told the police about that, but also that she'd never had a key to Mrs Lovelock's house. The only person apart from Nick and me who appears ever to have had one is Paul.'

'What about Mrs Redman?'

It is so easy to forget all the most obvious things. I had not thought of Mrs Redman.

'I should think she almost certainly had,' I said. 'She probably let herself in every morning.'

My own domestic help, that very smart young woman who came to me twice a week, had had a key to my house from the start and came and went as she chose.

'Do you know where Mrs Redman lives?' Felix asked.

'You mean you want to go and see her?' I said.

'I thought it might be useful.'

'But you don't think she could have doped Anna's milk.'

'It's unlikely, but it isn't impossible. She could have done it in the morning when she was working in the house, alone in the kitchen. She wouldn't have had to wait till Anna went out. The milk would have been delivered early, wouldn't it, and been put in the fridge?'

'That's absolute nonsense.'

'How d'you know? She may have nursed a bitter hatred of Anna over the years.'

'But she's such a nice woman.'

'Nicer than the Hearns? Nicer than Kimber? Nicer than Julia Bordman and all Mrs Lovelock's other friends?'

'I'm not sure she isn't.'

'Did she get a legacy from Mrs Lovelock?'

'I don't believe she did. Anyway, I haven't heard it mentioned.'

'And Anna did. Her five thousand a year may have sounded like riches to Mrs Redman. Yet Anna was really a servant of Mrs Lovelock's, like herself. It might have maddened Mrs Redman.'

'I don't believe it for a moment.'

'All the same, let's go and see her. You didn't say if you've got her address.'

I hadn't, but I knew the Redmans had a telephone and I found their address in the directory. They lived in a council house in a development on the edge of the town. Mr Redman was an electrician who worked for a firm in Allingford. I had never met him, but when we found the house and rung the bell and the door was opened by a short, bald man with what looked as if it was going to be a friendly smile, but which changed abruptly when he saw us to a suspicious frown, I assumed that that was who he was.

'Is Mrs Redman at home?' I asked. 'Can we see her?'

The frown deepened. 'If you're the police . . .' he said and paused. 'Are you police? She's had enough of them. She isn't feeling well.'

'No, I'm a friend of Mrs Lovelock's,' I said. 'I'm Mrs Freer. And this is my husband. Mrs Redman knows me.'

'What d'you want her for?' he asked. 'Like I said, she isn't feeling well. All this business of finding Miss Cox nearly dead and calling Dr Cairns and him calling the police, and them asking her question after question has been too much for her. She's lying down.'

But as if to contradict this statement a voice called through the open door of what was plainly the kitchen, 'What is it, Stephen?'

'All right then, come in,' he said, and as if once the invitation had been reluctantly given he felt that he had the duties of a host, the frown on his high, shining forehead disappeared and the smile that seemed more natural to his face returned.

He took us into a small, comfortably furnished room, or one which would have been comfortable if it had not been so unbelievably clean. Every surface that could be polished shone. The net curtains at the window looked as if they had just been washed. The pale cream carpet had not a single spot on it. I felt nervous of walking across it in case somehow I left footmarks. Mrs Redman came into the room a moment after us. She was taller than her husband and was slim in a firm, muscular way. She looked about fifty and had thick, curly hair that had turned grey, grey eyes and a broad, ruddy face. She was wearing navy blue slacks and a pale blue hand-knitted pullover.

Her husband said, 'I thought they was police and I said you'd had enough of them, but this lady said she was Mrs Freer and that you'd know her.'

'Of course I do,' she said. 'Hallo, Mrs Freer. Take a seat, won't you? And is this Mr Freer? What can I do for you?'

Felix replied and I was glad to leave it to him. 'We really won't keep you long, Mrs Redman. It's just that a question came up which we thought you might be able to answer. It's whether you had a key of your own to Mrs Lovelock's house, or did Miss Cox let you in when you arrived in the mornings? If you feel we're being inquisitive, it's because Miss Cox asked me down to Allingford to help investigate the murder of Miss Galvin. And now there's the problem of what happened to Miss Cox herself. But I'm not police. I'm a private detective.'

I could not remember that I had ever heard him make that claim before, but he said it earnestly, with a faint sound of apology in his voice.

'Oh, sit down, sit down, do!' she exclaimed and we both sat down obediently on the immaculately clean and un-crumpled cretonne-covered sofa. 'That's just what the police was asking me. Had I got a key? and when I said I hadn't, because Miss Cox was always up ever so early and used to let me in and we'd have a cup to tea together, they asked how did I get in this morning when she was in bed, dead to the world. So I told them about Mr Duffield's key.'

'Mr Duffield's?' Felix said. 'But didn't he take that with him when the police took him away? I mean, didn't he have a key-ring in his pocket, or something like that?'

She shook her head. 'You see, he was ever so careless and he knew he was, and when he lost the key Mrs Lovelock gave him and Miss Cox gave him a spare, he said he wouldn't take it with him but he'd hang it on a hook there was in the garage. And usually when he come home to the house he'd just ring the bell and Miss Cox or I would let him in. So when she didn't answer this morning when I arrived I had a feeling something was wrong and I went and took that key and let myself in and there she was in bed still and ever so pale and for a moment I thought she was dead. Oh, the shock, Mrs Freer! My sister-in-law died last May and that was a shock, but it was different. I mean, I'd been told she'd passed away before I went into the room and I had my brother with me. It wasn't like walking in on her by myself and finding she was gone when I wasn't expecting it. But then I saw Miss Cox was breathing and she felt quite warm and her eyes was closed, and if she'd been dead I believe they'd have been open, wouldn't they? Anyway, I run to the telephone and calls Dr Cairns and he come as quick as he could and he said it looked like she'd taken too many sleeping-pills, and then he stood there, thinking, and then he says, "Mrs Redman," he says, "I'm going to call the police." So that's what he done and a man called Superintendent Dawnay arrived and he and Dr Cairns had a long talk and then this superintendent asked me about the key and I told him what I've told you, and then the police took away a bottle from the fridge that had just the last drops of milk in it, and a saucepan there was in the sink. I was a bit puzzled by that saucepan, it wasn't

like Miss Cox to leave it there overnight without washing
it up and putting it away.'

Her swift, slightly breathless narrative came to an end.
She looked at Felix hopefully to see if she had told him
what he wanted.

'Thank you very much,' he said. 'That's very informa-
tive. So in fact anyone could have got into the house yesterday if they'd happened to know about the key in the garage.'

'I suppose they could,' she said.

'Do you by any chance know who might have known?'

She shook her head. 'I don't know what Mr Duffield, or
even Miss Cox may have said to anyone about it.'

'And that key he lost, you don't know anything about
where he may have done that?'

'All I know is he'd been into town and thought he must
have pulled it out with a handkerchief when he took it out
of a pocket.'

'I see. Well, we won't take up any more of your time.
I'm sorry to have troubled you.'

'You're welcome.'

I wondered if she had told the police they were welcome
when they questioned her, but it seemed unlikely. Her husband saw us out of the house and stood in the doorway,
watching us until he saw us get into Felix's car and drive
away.

I expected him to drive home and when he took what I
thought was a wrong turning, I told him so.

He said, 'Isn't this the way to Morebury Close?'

'Is that where we're going?' I asked.

'Yes, I thought we'd see if we can speak to Anna,' he
said.

'About the key?'

'Among other things.'

I remembered that that was what he had said when I
had asked him why he had gone to see Dr Cairns.

'Those pills again, I suppose,' I said. 'But if it wasn't attempted suicide, and you seem to be sure it wasn't, do you think she's going to be able to tell you anything about them?'

'You can't tell till you've tried. You didn't think there was any point in going to see Mrs Redman, yet look how illuminating it was.'

'It means that when Dawnay asked me if I'd ever had the key in my possession, he already knew about that key in the garage. But it suggests, doesn't it, that whoever doped Anna's milk wasn't the same person as the one who got in and shot Kate, because whoever did that could have made use of the garage key, he wouldn't have had to smash a window.'

Felix drove for some minutes in silence. Then he observed, 'I've never really believed in that smashed window, you know. I've had a feeling all along it was done after the murder of Kate to make it look as if the intruder got in from outside, when in fact he'd got quietly into the house by the door.'

'So after all you're thinking of Nick. Anna isn't going to thank you.'

'Yes, it's true I was thinking of him until I heard about the key he lost. But together with the key in the garage, that's broadened the field somewhat.'

'Are you going to talk about it to her?'

'I'll see. We don't even know what condition she'll be in or if we'll be able to see her.' He was silent again and I did not feel inclined to go on questioning him, as I felt it would lead nowhere. We were turning into Morebury Close before he exclaimed bitterly, 'I don't *like* that key! Things were simple before, but now they're complicated.'

Things had not seemed specially simple to me unless the Hearns and Paul Kimber had been acting together, which might have made sense if I could have thought of any possible reason why they should have done so, since Margot had a supply of the relevant drug and Paul had a key to the bungalow. But according to Felix the key was not important.

We turned into Mrs Lovelock's drive and got out of the car and rang the bell. The door was opened almost immediately by Nick Duffield.

CHAPTER 8

He was pale and looked tense and uneasy, not at all like
the young man who had offered me wine when I had arrived
at the bungalow after Mrs Lovelock's funeral. A funeral
may not be the most cheerful of occasions, but probably it
puts less strain on the nervous system than a couple of days
of being questioned by the police about a murder which
one may or may not have committed.

He said, 'Oh, it's you.' He did not sound exactly relieved,
but at least indifferent. 'Come in.' He held the door open
until we were inside, then let it close with a light slam. 'I
thought it might be the police again.'

'Haven't they finished with you?' I asked.

'Do they ever finish with you? God knows how many
times I've answered the same questions. They've let me go
because if they'd held me any longer they'd have had to
charge me with something, and they've no evidence against
me, but that's no guarantee they aren't going to keep after
me.'

'Didn't they let you go because you couldn't have been
the person who doped Anna's milk?' I said.

'That may have had something to do with it. It's a fine
thing to have an alibi no one can question.' He sounded
bitter and sullen. 'I'm leaving for Australia just as soon as
I can. I've got to stay till after the inquest, but then I'm
going and I'm not coming back. I've had enough of
Europe.'

'How is Anna?' I asked.

'She seems all right.' He still sounded indifferent.

'Can we see her?'

'I'll ask her.'

'Are the nurse and the policewoman still here?'

'No, they've gone. And I'm only hanging around because I don't like the idea of leaving her alone, but if you can stay with her . . .' It seemed suddenly to occur to him that he did not know who the man was whom he had let into the house with me. 'Are you the police?' he asked Felix.

'He's my husband,' I said, surprised that I had forgotten that the two of them had not yet met. 'Anna knows him. But where d'you want to go?'

'I want to do what I tried to do the other evening,' he answered. 'I want to go to London to see Bairnsfather tomorrow. I've made an appointment to see him at nine o'clock. And at least there's no fog now. If I hadn't got worried about driving in that damned fog along roads I didn't know, which made me turn back, I'd have been in London by the time of the murder and no one could have tried to pin it on me. This climate! I tell you, there's nothing about this country I like.'

'I believe strong winds and heavy rain are forecast,' Felix observed.

I doubted if he had actually listened to a weather bulletin, but I realized that he had taken one of his swift and not necessarily rational dislikes to Nick Duffield, which would make him happy to pin the murder on him if he could think of a way of doing so. He was gazing at Nick with a sort of blank thoughtfulness which meant that he was thinking hard about something or other, though it was not necessarily of Nick.

I felt sorry for Nick, remembering the good-humoured charm that he had had before the experiences of the last few days.

'About Anna.' I said. 'Will you ask her if we can go in to see her? She's still in bed, is she?'

'I don't think so,' he said. 'But she's in her room. Wait a minute.'

He knocked at the door of the room which I knew was
Anna's, went in and after a moment came out again and
said, 'OK, she'll see you.'

We both went into the room.

Anna was in the easy chair by the window, wearing the
purple quilted dressing-gown and the velvet slippers that I
had noticed the last time that I had been in the room. The
strong purple made her face look greyish. Her eyes looked
unusually large and dull and her cheeks fallen in. But the
bed was made and the room was as tidy as it had been
before. I hoped that the nurse or the WPC had seen to that
before leaving and not left it to Anna to straighten things
to her liking. Not that it might not have helped her to do
it, for to sit simply idle, doing nothing, was so unlike her.
There was a tray with coffee on it on the low table before
her. She managed to greet us with a vague smile as we
came in.

'I thought somehow you'd be coming round soon,' she
said. 'Do sit down. Would you like a drink? I'm not allowed
to have one, so I've just been drinking coffee. Cup after
cup. Dear Nick's been making it for me. But now I've
finished what there was so I can't offer you any, but Nick
can get you some whisky or whatever you like, if you'll open
the door again, Felix, and call him.'

'Don't bother,' I said. 'We don't want anything. We just
came to see how you were.'

'I'm all right, quite all right, though a bit swimmy,' she
said. 'I understand I didn't have enough of the stuff to
need a stomach pump, but somehow nothing seems real. I
suppose I haven't got it out of my system yet. I'm going to
feel rather scared after this of taking my pills in the way I
have for years. I know that's stupid. I need my pills. But I
could drop the milk, I suppose, then I could be sure of what
I was taking. Not that anyone is going to try the same thing
twice, would you think? If someone really wants me out of

the way they'll have to try something else next time.'

'I don't believe anyone wants you out of the way,' I said. 'They just wanted to be dead sure you'd be sound asleep while they searched the house. You know about the search, don't you?'

Felix and I both sat down.

She gave a melancholy little laugh. 'I do indeed. Almost the moment I opened my eyes the police were at me, asking what anyone could have been searching for. And I couldn't tell them a thing. I know I was still pretty confused, but really I couldn't, Virginia. You know I've lived in this house for over twenty years and I thought I knew about everything that was in it, literally everything. As you know, Helen made me handle all her business for her, paying bills, writing to the accountant about her income tax, sometimes typing letters she dictated to me because her hands had got too shaky for her to be able to write as nicely as she wanted, and all that sort of thing, and still I couldn't think of anything that anyone could have wanted. But it's true my mind isn't very clear yet, so perhaps I'll think of something later.'

'I don't suppose you've had any chance yet to check if your intruder perhaps found what he was looking for,' Felix said.

She thought that over for a moment, then shook her head.

'No, it's true I haven't. I haven't been out of this room yet, except to the bathroom. There's one thing I did check, though. In the bathroom. My pills. I keep them in the cupboard there and the bottle's nearly full. I've taken a few in the normal way since Dr Cairns gave me my last lot, but there aren't enough missing to have done me any damage. So that means something, doesn't it?'

'That someone brought in the pills they put in your milk and didn't rely on your own supply,' Felix said. 'I should have guessed that was how it happened anyway.'

I thought of Margot, telling me she took the same pills as Anna. But they were not an uncommon brand, so far as I knew. Probably any number of people took them, at least occasionally.

'Is Nick really going up to London this evening and leaving you on your own?' I asked.

'Yes, but it's all right, I don't mind,' she answered. 'Mrs Redman's going to come in presently to stay with me. She rang up just a few minutes ago. She said you'd been to see her and asked her about the key in the garage, just as the police did, and that made her worry in case whoever's got it uses it to come in again. I told her that was most unlikely as I think the police took it away with them, but anyway, she's coming. She's such a good soul. So don't worry about me.'

'And you really can't think of anything anyone could have wanted?' Felix said.

'I really can't.'

'I believe there was a packet of what Virginia thought were letters, which Duffield threw in the fire,' he said. 'Could they have been of any interest to anyone?'

'Oh, those.' She frowned. 'I don't know. I don't think so. I think they were just a few letters he'd written to Helen. Perhaps they were written when he was most upset about the deaths of his parents. That might have made him want to burn them.'

'And there wasn't perhaps some photograph someone wanted to get hold of?'

'Something somehow compromising?' she asked.

'I wasn't thinking of anything definite,' he said.

'Well, I don't know of anything like that. Helen had lots of photographs of her dogs, but they weren't hidden.' She looked from Felix to me, then back to Felix. I had a feeling that at that moment she almost told us something, then decided against it. She was silent for a moment, then said,

'It's very good of you to be troubling about it all. I do appreciate it. And tonight I'll see that Mrs Redman makes sure that the bolts on all the doors are shot, as well as turning the keys inside. I'm not sure if she's staying the night, or just looking in, but in any case, don't worry about me.'

'You wouldn't like to come home with us?' I suggested. 'We've the car here and I've a little room where you could sleep. Why don't you do that, Anna?'

She looked less pleased than I thought that she should at the invitation, but then she summoned up a smile.

'That's really sweet of you, and just like you, but honestly I'd sooner just stay here quietly,' she said. 'As I said, the police have taken away the key that was in the garage, and anyway, no one's going to try the same thing twice. And Mrs Redman's going to make me some soup or something presently.'

It began to seem to me that she wanted to get rid of us. I stood up and kissed her, thinking that after all visitors are not always really welcome when one is feeling sufficiently unwell. When they first appear it seems splendid that they should be concerned enough to make the visit, but very quickly their mere presence can become excessively tiring. We said goodbye to her and left the room. Just outside it, as if he had been waiting there for us, we found Nick Duffield. He was carrying a small suitcase.

'You're leaving, are you?' he said. 'I thought you'd be staying with her.'

'She didn't seem to want us to stay,' I answered.

'Then perhaps I'd better not go yet.' He looked put out. 'She isn't really fit to be left alone.'

'She said Mrs Redman's coming soon,' I said. 'She can take care of her.'

'But I'd better wait at least until she gets here.' He put the suitcase down on the floor. 'Of course I needn't really go till tomorrow, but I feel the police are going to be after me again if I don't get moving soon. I want to put as much distance between me and them as quickly as I can manage. Not that they won't be able to pick me up in London if they want to, but at least I'd have the illusion of being free for a little while, and if they have some bother finding me, that'll be my pleasure. But I'll wait till Mrs Redman gets here.'

Felix was gazing at him with the same blank stare as before, but he said nothing. We let ourselves out at the door.

In the drive he said, 'I wonder why he's in such a hurry to get to London.'

'Don't you think it's more or less as he said, he's taken a dislike to our Mr Dawnay and wants to get away from him?' I said. 'I think in his place I'd feel the same. But, Felix, did you get a feeling at all that Anna actually has some suspicion of what the intruder was looking for last night? I think there was a moment when she almost told us.'

'Oh yes,' he said, as if that were a matter of course. 'She certainly knows.'

'If so, you'd think she'd have told the police about it. She might not tell us because she might think it wasn't our business, but she'd have told the police.'

'Possibly.'

'You don't think so.'

'On the whole, no, though I don't know any more about it than you do. But she got me down here to investigate a murder, and if she's really got anything to tell me about it, you'd think she'd tell me at least as much as she'd tell the police. So as she hasn't told me anything, perhaps she hasn't told them either.'

'You know, I don't think she cares so very much about who did the murder,' I said. 'What she really wants is to see Nick cleared of it. And he's free now, so she may be suggesting soon you should go home.'

'I'm sure she will.' He slipped an arm through mine. 'What do you say to dinner at the Rose and Crown?'

I would have agreed, but we had just reached the gate and there, apparently waiting for us, was Paul Kimber and before I could answer he said, with his teeth flashing in his beard in a warm smile, 'Hallo. What about coming in next door for a drink?'

So the matter of dinner was postponed for the moment and we went with Paul into his bungalow.

It was about half the size of Mrs Lovelock's and unlike the garden, which was beautifully kept, it had a weather-beaten and neglected look. It must have been a long time since any painting had been done on its woodwork. Inside there seemed to be traces of Paul's hobbies everywhere. It was moderately clean, but gardening catalogues were scattered about in most available places. There were a few pieces of agate and crystal lying mixed up with heaps of typing paper. There was a typewriter on the floor. He used his garage, I knew, for the actual work on his jewellery, leaving his car outside to suffer what rain might fall. The furniture was old and shabby, though an odd little table and a chair or two looked as if they might be antiques of some value. The pictures were Paul's own not very inspiring watercolours, most of them of scenes that I recognized in the surrounding countryside. A fire was buring in the brick grate.

He waved us to chairs, asked us what we would like to drink, brought bottles out of a corner cupboard, gave us our drinks, then, as Felix lit a cigarette, sat down on the floor between us and looked from one to the other of us with his bright smile.

'Well?' he said. 'Well?'

'Well what?' I asked.

'Do you think I had anything to do with it?' He seemed to enjoy the thought that perhaps we did.

'With doping Anna?' I said.

He nodded earnestly. 'I can get in and out of that house whenever I want to, you know. I've had a key for years.'

'So why didn't you use it when you went in to murder Kate?'

'Ah, I was hoping you'd ask that,' he said. 'I've been trying to think it out myself. The obvious answer is that I did use it, then smashed the kitchen window after I'd left to make it look as if someone else had come in from outside.'

'I do wish people would stop accusing themselves of that murder,' Felix said. 'It's wearisome.'

'We only do it because we're all frightened,' Paul said. 'We want to make it sound absurd. About the emeralds . . .' He paused again and looked questioningly from Felix to me. 'Suppose there were some real emeralds somewhere that the ones I was given to have mended were a copy of. That's sometimes done, you know, with really valuable jewellery. Then the real ones are kept in the bank except for very special occasions, and only the fake ones get worn.' His smile disappeared and he suddenly looked serious. 'I'm not saying that's how it was, but only that it's something to think about. Naturally if there's anything in it, the police will have the ones in the bank by now.'

Felix shook his head. 'The idea doesn't appeal to me.'

'Why not?'

'For one thing, I'm sure Anna would have been sure to know about it, and besides that, why should anyone bother with stealing the false necklace if he happened to know there was a genuine one somewhere?'

'And he'd have had to be something of an expert to be able to spot right away that the stones in the one taken from the safe on the night of the murder weren't genuine, and so just throw it away,' Paul said. 'I see that. And I

don't know of any real expert around, unless by any chance
—have you thought of it?—it might be Duffield.'

'He's got the best alibi anyone can have for last night,' I
said. 'He was in the hands of the police.'

'But suppose he had an accomplice. How much do we
really know about Nick Duffield?'

Felix showed signs of interest. 'D'you know, that's something I've been asking myself? And I shouldn't be surprised
if the police have been asking themselves that too. I believe
he was about twelve or thirteen when he was taken to Australia and it's about twenty years later that he came back.
A lot can happen to a person in twenty years. We don't
really know anything about the sort of company he used to
keep there. But I'd forget the emeralds, if I were you. I
think they're only a red herring. About sleeping-pills, do
you take them?'

'Never in my life,' Paul said.

'Dr Cairns has never prescribed them for you?'

'Never.'

'Did you know about the key to Mrs Lovelock's house
that was kept in her garage?'

Paul looked puzzled. 'No, I don't think I ever heard
about that. I thought I had the only spare key there was.
But if there was a key out there . . .' He paused again for
a moment and thought. 'It means that anybody—I mean
anybody—could have got in.'

'Oh, forget the key,' Felix said. 'Another red herring.'

'I don't believe you,' Paul said. 'I think it might be
important.'

'Well, perhaps it is in its way.' Felix tossed his cigarette
stub into the fire. 'Virginia, if we're going to have that
dinner we were talking about, we ought to be going.'

'No, wait a moment,' Paul said as we both stood up.
'What do you mean by that—that it may be important *in
its way*?'

'I'm not sure that I know myself,' Felix answered. 'Does it make sense to say that a thing's important because it's unimportant?'

Paul got to his feet from the floor, not quite as easily as he had sat down on it. He had only to become a little older and a little more corpulent to find it advisable to drop the habit of sitting there.

'You mean it seems so very unimportant that it must mean something?' he said.

'Something like that.'

But I was not at all sure that that was what Felix had meant. In fact, I was not sure that he had meant anything at all. He wanted to sound baffling and mysterious. That suited the rôle that he was playing. We thanked Paul for the drinks and went out to the car.

In the end we did not go to the Rose and Crown for dinner, because when we arrived home, where I wanted to go to change my dress and put on a little fresh make-up before setting out for the evening, we found that we had a visitor. Of all unexpected people, it was Charlie. By himself too. He was standing at my front door, looking at it in a forlorn sort of way, as if he thought that it might open of itself if he looked at it hard enough. A car that I recognized as Julia's was at my gate. It surprised me as much as finding Charlie there alone.

'Hallo, Charlie,' I said, 'I didn't know you could drive.'

'Oh yes, I've been doing it for years,' he answered. 'It's really quite easy once you know how.'

'I hope we haven't kept you waiting for too long,' I said. 'We went to see Anna.'

'I don't think I've been waiting very long,' he replied. 'I thought I'd wait a bit in case you came back. There's something special I want to tell you about.'

'Come in, then.' I unlocked the door, pushed it open and we went in.

I then had a nasty shock. As Felix followed Charlie and me into the house, he put a hand into a pocket and brought out a small glass owl which I recognized at once. I knew that it was Steuben glass and that Kate had brought it from America as a present to her aunt on one of her rare visits. It had stood on the table in Mrs Lovelock's hall, next to her telephone, but it must somehow have found its way into Felix's pocket during the few minutes that we had stood there, talking to Nick. I knew how deft Felix could be at appropriating anything that took his fancy without being observed, but usually he could be relied on not to practise this skill of his in the houses of friends. So this could only mean, I thought, either that his moral sense had deteriorated even further than when I had seen him last, or else that he did not think of the heirs of Mrs Lovelock as friends.

He put the owl down beside my telephone. It was really a very charming thing. He smiled at me and said, 'Nice, isn't it?'

'No,' I said.

'Oh yes,' he said. 'Very nice indeed.'

'It's going straight back to Morebury Close.'

He shook his head. 'Be reasonable. If I'd managed to get down a day sooner you know Anna would have wanted me to choose a memento of Mrs Lovelock, and this is what I'd have chosen.'

'There wasn't any reason why you should have come down a day sooner,' I said. 'There hadn't been a murder. Nick hadn't been taken off for questioning. No one would have thought of asking you to come down specially just to help yourself to something.'

'But suppose I'd happened to be staying with you, as I occasionally do, of course Anna would have invited me to come. I can't think what you're making a fuss about. I mean it for you, of course. I'm not taking it away with me.'

He could sound dreadfully reasonable when he gave his mind to it. Everything that he had said was almost true.

'If you leave it here I'll be taking it back to Anna tomorrow and saying there's been a mistake made,' I said.

'She'll only tell you to keep it.'

She almost certainly would, even if she could not quite understand how it had got into my possession.

Charlie was looking puzzled. 'Don't you like it?' he asked me. 'I've always liked it. It's what I'd have chosen when we went to Mrs Lovelock's to choose something to remember her by, unless perhaps it was those china dogs she had, but my mother said someone else wanted those and she brought away just a glass paperweight I don't care for much. But if we couldn't have the dogs, I'd have chosen this little owl.'

'Then take it,' I said, picking it up and thrusting it into his hands. 'Take it away, for God's sake. And if anyone asks where you got it from, tell them I gave it to you.' I did not want Julia or anyone else wondering if Charlie could somehow have helped himself to it.

'That's awfully nice of you,' he said. 'Thanks.'

'Now come in here, Charlie, and tell me why you wanted to see me.' I led the way into the sitting-room.

He sat down in a chair near the gas fire, which I lit. He caressed the owl gently between his hands.

'It's only that I'm worried about what I ought to do with a key I found,' he said.

'Another key!' I exploded. 'We've been hearing enough about keys.'

The puzzled look returned to his face. 'Don't you want me to tell you about it? I thought you would.'

'Yes, of course, Charlie—I'm sorry,' I said. 'What is it you want to tell me?'

'It's that I found a key in one of our chairs at home,' he

said. 'Down beside the cushion in it, you know, where it's
so awfully easy to lose things. I've sometimes found very
interesting things down beside those cushions, letters and
bills and handkerchiefs and once a piece of toast with some
jam on it. I don't know how that got there. It was rather
sticky and not really very nice. But I found the key the day
after Mr Duffield came in to have tea with my mother. I
remember he sneezed and I said I hoped he wasn't getting
a cold, and he pulled his handkerchief out of his pocket in
a hurry, and that's when I think the key fell out and slipped
down beside the cushion. And I found it next day and I
rather liked having it. I don't know why, but I like keys.
I've quite a collection of them. But I don't say anything
about it to my mother, because she thinks it's silly to collect
them. But then the police came to see her and they kept
asking her if she'd got a key to Mrs Lovelock's house, and
of course she said she hadn't, and I didn't like to say perhaps the one they wanted was the one I'd got, because I
didn't think they'd believe me about how I'd found it and
they might think she'd really taken it and be angry with
her. But I've been worrying about it ever since, because if
the police want it I know I ought to give it to them, only
I'm a bit afraid of them. They might think my wanting to
keep the key for my collection was a bit peculiar and if ever
I do anything too peculiar they might take me away. It's
very bad to be peculiar, you know.'

'And so you brought the key to me so that I could give
it to the police,' I said.

'Well, I heard that man Mr Dawnay say he'd been talking to you, so I knew you knew him and I thought if you said
you'd picked it up somewhere he'd believe you.' Charlie
brought a Yale latch-key out of a pocket. 'Do you think you
could give it to him without saying anything about my
collection?'

'I'll do my best.' I accepted the key and put it into the

handbag that I had put down on the floor beside me. 'But tell me something, Charlie. Did you know that a key to Mrs Lovelock's house was kept in her garage?'

'In her garage?' he said. 'What a funny place to keep a key. Or do you mean it was her car-keys?'

'No, it was a key to her house.'

'Then anyone who wanted to could get into her house whenever they liked, couldn't they? Unless, of course, she kept the garage locked. We always keep ours locked. My mother's very particular about it. But if Mrs Lovelock did, the key inside it wouldn't be any use to anyone, would it?'

I caught Felix's eye. He was grinning a little as if it amused him that it had taken Charlie, in his simplicity, to ask this fairly obvious question. For if the garage had been locked on the evening of Kate's death, it meant, of course, that the murderer might really have needed to smash the kitchen window in order to get into the house. Not that that point was likely to have escaped Detective-Superintendent Dawnay, even if it had not occurred to me. But then something else did occur to me.

'Felix, Mrs Redman talked about that key being kept in the garage,' I said, 'but Mrs Lovelock had twin garages, one for her car and one for Anna's. And if the key was kept in Mrs Lovelock's, then it was almost certainly unlocked, because Nick would have taken her car, not Anna's, when he drove off to London, and almost certainly he wouldn't have locked it behind him when he drove out. But if the key was kept in Anna's garage, she probably did lock it behind her when she got home after coming to us here. So isn't it important to find out in which garage the key was kept? Oughtn't we to ask Anna?'

'I've said, forget the key,' Felix answered.

'But why?'

'For one thing, because it's the kind of thing the police

can sort out for themselves without any help from us. If I'm to be any help, I've got to approach the whole problem differently. What I want at the moment is to know more about Duffield, not about the key he lost.'

'Then don't you think this key I found is important?' Charlie asked eagerly. 'Would it be all right if I had it back for my collection?'

I hesitated and Felix said, 'Perhaps we'd better keep it for the moment, Charlie.'

'I can tell you something about Mr Duffield,' Charlie said.

'You can?' Felix said.

'Yes, he's not a nice man. He's a very bad man.'

'What makes you say that?'

'I don't like to repeat it.'

Felix nodded, as if he respected this reticence. But then he said, 'I think you could tell us in confidence. In the strictest confidence.'

Charlie wriggled in his chair. 'I don't like to say it with a lady present.'

'You needn't worry about her. She's used to it.'

Charlie gave me a glance, looking deeply embarrassed.

'He was very rude to my mother,' he said at last. 'He said she was a nosey bitch.'

'Dear me, that wasn't very nice of him,' Felix said.

'I thought it was very, very rude. And his ears too, I think they're rather strange. Have you noticed his ears? I didn't know ears could grow.'

Felix did not attempt to solve the problem of what Charlie meant about Nick Duffield's ears. I had never noticed anything strange about them myself.

'Did he say what your mother was nosey about?' Felix asked.

'It was something to do with Mrs Lovelock's money. I didn't really understand it.'

'Had your mother said anything about Mrs Lovelock's money?'

'I don't know. I get muddled about money. My mother doesn't give me very much for myself. When I have it I like to buy keys for my collection. But she doesn't like me to do that. It's like wine. I like it, but I never buy it, because she says it might make me make a fool of myself. But I had some after Mrs Lovelock's funeral and I didn't make a fool of myself, did I, Mrs Freer?'

'No, Charlie, you were quite all right,' I answered.

'Of course I believe I showed how beautiful I thought Miss Galvin was, and that may have been because of the wine, but I didn't even know it was Miss Galvin. I know she didn't like me, so if I'd known who it was—'

He was interrupted by the ringing of the doorbell.

I went to the front door and found Julia on the doorstep. She was in an unbuttoned anorak and an old tartan skirt. Her hair was dishevelled. A taxi was just disappearing down the road.

'He's here, isn't he, Virginia?' she asked, almost falling in at the door in her anxiety. 'That's our car in the road. He *is* here, isn't he?'

'Yes, and he's quite all right,' I said. I put an arm round her shoulders as she looked as if she were in need of support. 'He's just been chatting to us.'

'Thank God!' she exclaimed. 'I was so scared. You see, I lay down in the afternoon and went to sleep and when I got up I couldn't find him and then I found he'd taken the car. I wish I'd never taught him to drive it. Of course he's never had a licence, but he wanted to learn so badly and he has so few pleasures, so I used to let him have a go on quiet side roads. I didn't know where he'd gone today, but I thought it might be to you, as he's always liked you, and I know he's been worrying about something the last few days, though I don't think for a moment he understands what's happened.'

I drew her into the sitting-room.

'Here's your mother, Charlie,' I said. 'She couldn't think what had become of you.'

'I'm sorry, Mother,' he said. 'You were asleep, you see, and I didn't want to wake you up when I decided I ought to go out.'

'I was so afraid he'd gone to the police,' Julia said to Felix and me, as usual talking as if Charlie himself were not there. 'I've been afraid he'd do that ever since all these troubles started. I know he's been wanting to do it.'

'But why?' I asked.

'To confess to these crimes,' Julia said. 'He's always confessing to crimes. He thinks people like him to do it. But I was so terribly afraid they might actually believe him.'

CHAPTER 9

I said, 'I don't think they'd believe him for a moment.'

'Why not?' Julia said. 'Wouldn't they have been glad to have the whole thing cleared up by someone confessing?'

'They'd more probably have been irritated,' I said. 'People are always causing them trouble, when there's been something like a murder, by confessing to things they couldn't possibly have done.'

'But Charlie could have done it,' she said.

'What on earth do you mean?'

'Well, he was there—I'm sure you know that—when I went in to choose that stupid remembrance of poor Helen, and he could have slipped in at the door when no one was looking and put the poison in Boz's dish. And then he could have driven back in the evening in spite of the fog—not many people know he can drive, so no one would think of him—and—' She dropped suddenly into a chair and hid her face in her hands. 'I think I'm going mad,' she muttered. 'I know it's all nonsense. He hadn't any poison, or a gun, and he hadn't any sleeping-pills to give Anna.'

'Of course not,' I said.

'But I know who murdered Kate Galvin,' Charlie remarked.

Julia dropped her hands and raised her head quickly. There was a flush on her pale cheeks. 'You *what*?'

'I know who murdered Kate Galvin,' he repeated calmly. 'I heard her say so.'

'Who?' I asked.

'Mrs Hearn. She and Mr Hearn came and talked to me while I was waiting in the car, and when they were leaving me to go into the house I heard her say distinctly, "If that bloody woman's still here—" I beg your pardon, Mrs Freer, I know it's not a nice word, but she said it. "If that bloody woman's still here, I'll murder her, see if I don't." '

Julia gave a shudder, then a deep sigh, then said softly, with a tenderness I had not heard in her voice before, 'Oh, Charlie.'

'But it's quite true, I heard her say it, I'm not making it up,' he said.

'Of course you aren't, only, you see, she didn't quite mean it as you thought.' She looked up at me with a slight smile. 'As a matter of fact, it makes me more inclined to believe Margot had nothing to do with the murder than anything I've heard yet. I've had my suspicions of her, you know, because of all of us who were there that evening she hated Kate the most. And I've thought about Roderick too, and wondered if when he made a joke here yesterday evening about Kate having some information on him that she could use to damage him, there mightn't have been something in it. A joke can be a very good thing to hide behind. But I've realized that I could be suspected too, and that's why I was really so scared when I thought Charlie might have gone to the police. I thought they might have thought he was confessing to protect me. Perhaps I was wrong when I said Margot hated Kate the most. Perhaps I hated her even more. I've tried to get over it, because I know she was only a child when she lied about Charlie, but I've never managed to forgive her. You see, the suspicion of what he's supposed to have done has clung to him all his life. The story of it got around somehow, and I've seen people looking at him, particularly if there were young children there, as if he were a monster. And he's the most innocent soul there ever was. Now, Charlie dear, we're going. You really shouldn't have driven off in the car without telling me where you were going.'

'I'm sorry,' he said, then turned to me and said, 'I'm

sorry I've taken up your time, Mrs Freer.' To Felix he added, 'Goodbye, Mr Freer.'

'Just a minute, Mrs Bordman,' Felix said. 'I wonder if you could explain something. Your son told us that on some occasion when Duffield was in your house he used the expression about you that you were a nosey bitch. If that's true, would you mind if I ask you what he thought you were nosey about?'

Julia looked shocked, then began to look angry, then changed her mind and laughed.

'Yes, I remember it,' she said. 'That young man has atrocious manners, but perhaps it was my own fault. You see, I'd been spending an afternoon with Mrs Lovelock and she'd been talking about Nick, talking about how wonderful it was to have him home and how good and kind he was, and how she hoped he'd stay for as long as she lasted. Of course, she knew that wouldn't be long, and she talked about how she was going to leave her money divided between him and Kate, and somehow I got irritated by all that praise of a very ordinary young man, and I said something about its being possible that he'd come home just to get her money and hadn't she ever asked herself that. I know it wasn't very nice of me, but it was as if she'd never thought of such a thing herself, because she seemed to take me much more seriously than I meant, and she said perhaps she ought to think it over before she really made up her mind, what she ought to do. And then she must have told Nick something about what I'd said, because he came to see me and told me straight out I was a nosey bitch. And perhaps he was right. I've never been too good at minding my own business.' She laughed again. 'Now we really must go.'

With Charlie carefully nursing his Steuben owl, he and she left together.

When they had gone I picked up my handbag, took out

the key that Charlie had given me and said, 'I forgot this. We might have told Julia about it, or given it back to Charlie for his collection.'

'What's the significance of collecting keys?' Felix asked. 'I'm sure they're symbolic of something.'

'Oh, very obviously symbolic,' I said. 'According to what I remember of my Freud, they're penis symbols.'

'And the poor chap's probably impotent, and though perhaps he did frighten her somehow, Kate's story about him was quite likely a lie. But if it's stuck to him, I don't wonder his mother hated her. But d'you know something that seems to me distinctly odd? The dear friends of Mrs Lovelock's who were invited to her home to choose remembrances of her all seem to have had excellent reasons for hating Kate. Was that just by chance, do you think?'

'I didn't hate her,' I said.

'No, I was forgetting about you.'

'And I don't think Paul did either.'

'I wonder if he really didn't. Now what are we going to eat, since it's a bit late to go to the Rose and Crown?'

We had omelettes presently, made by Felix, who is much better at making them than I am. But before he got around to doing it, we helped ourselves to sherry and for a time sat quietly in the sitting-room, not talking to each other any more, and as far as I was concerned, hardly thinking of the events of the day. It felt pleasant to have an almost blank mind. I found myself overcome by the kind of tiredness that can develop very suddenly and which makes it feel normal to slip away into sleep, and I might have done so if, after he had smoked one or two more cigarettes, Felix had not spoken. He spoke softly, as if it might have been to himself as much as to me, but when I opened my eyes, which had been closing, I saw him lying stretched out on the sofa with his eyes closed.

'Virginia, have you never thought seriously about committing a crime?' he asked.

I yawned before I answered. 'Not very seriously, no, I don't think so.'

'Why not?'

'I suppose I've never been sufficiently tempted,' I said.

'What do you think might tempt you?'

'I don't know. Perhaps shortage of money. Perhaps hatred. But the fact is, I've always had enough money to get by. I know nothing about the effects of acute poverty. And I've never hated anyone enough to want to damage them.'

'Not even me?'

He had opened his eyes, but was watching the smoke that he had just blown out and that was hanging above him, and was not looking at me.

'No, I can't help it, I'm rather fond of you,' I said.

'But didn't you hate me for a time?'

'For a little while, perhaps, when it first dawned on me that I couldn't stand our marriage after I'd such high hopes of it. But I never thought of murdering you, if that's what you're going to ask me next.'

'Not even in your imagination? Not even in fantasy?'

'I thought you asked me if I'd ever thought seriously of committing a crime.'

'So in your imagination you did.'

'Not even that really. There were times when I thought how helpful it would be if you simply didn't exist, but I don't think I ever saw myself doing anything about it.'

'And what about other crimes? Fraud, for instance. Hasn't the thought of that ever had any fascination for you?'

'It just scares me, I'm afraid. I feel sure I'd be caught. I think you must be very clever to carry out a successful fraud.'

'Haven't you ever even cheated on Income Tax?'

'Oh, I wouldn't like to say that for sure. But if I have, it's probably been mostly incompetence, not deliberate. The forms they send one are so incomprehensible, and I can't really afford an accountant and when I've relied on my bank they've made a hopeless mess of it. Have you noticed how nearly all the forms one gets sent nowadays about anything whatever are absolutely incomprehensible? The people who concoct them don't ever seem to have learnt English. They turn the meaning of words upside down and . . .' I stopped. 'What are we really talking about?'

'Murder,' Felix said.

I gave a deep sigh. I did not want to talk about it, though somehow I had known that that was what he would say.

'How could fraud have had anything to do with Kate's murder?' I asked. 'Nick might have wanted to get his hands on her money. He's the only person who's benefited by her death. But if he did, he went about things in a fearfully clumsy way.'

Felix stubbed out his cigarette. 'Did no one ever ask if Mrs Lovelock's death was entirely natural?'

I expect I looked stupid as I stared at him.

'So far as I know, they never did,' I said. 'Anyway, I know Nick couldn't have had anything to do with it. He was out somewhere, playing golf or something, when she died. It was Anna who found her, and she'd been out too. I know she was very distressed that Mrs Lovelock had been alone when she died.'

'It's sometimes said that if there's been a murder, the person who reports finding the body is the likeliest suspect.'

'But Anna certainly didn't benefit by Mrs Lovelock's death. Her life with her was perfectly comfortable, I should think, but if she died Anna knew that she was only going to inherit an annuity of five thousand a year. Nick's promised to pay for her in a good home for old people, but she couldn't have known beforehand that he was going to do that.'

'Are you sure about that golf?'

'It may not have been golf, but I do know he wasn't in the house when Mrs Lovelock died, and Dr Cairns had no hesitation about signing the death certificate.'

'Ah, Dr Cairns!'

I had finished my sherry and put down my glass. 'Why do you say, "Ah, Dr Cairns!" in that way?'

'He does seem to keep cropping up, doesn't he?'

'Do you think there's anything wrong about him? You went to see him yourself earlier today. Why was that?'

'Partly about those sleeping-pills he's been giving Anna, but I told you he wouldn't say anything about them. And while I was there I asked him about my left eye. It keeps watering and I thought perhaps the tear-duct had got blocked and it might be syringed. But I'm not registered with him and he only gave me a few minutes.'

I had seen no sign since he had arrived that his left eye had been watering and I felt sure that he had not told me the real reason why he had gone to see Dr Cairns.

'You don't really think there can have been anything suspicious about Mrs Lovelock's death, do you?' I said.

'Probably not,' he answered. 'If you aren't left to die in peace at eighty-eight it seems a little hard. Now about those omelettes, have you anything to go with them? An absolutely plain omelette made of eggs and nothing else isn't the most exciting thing in the world.'

'There are some mushrooms on the bottom shelf of the fridge.'

'Excellent.' He swung his legs to the ground. But he did not stand up immediately. His posture suddenly became rigid and his gaze settled on my face with a startled intensity, yet not as if he were really seeing me. He struck both his knees with his fists. 'Of course!' he said.

I waited for him to say something more, but he only sat there, staring at me in that bland fashion until I said, 'Of course mushrooms will help, but I've never thought of them as all that wonderful.'

'Mushrooms?' he said. 'What are you talking about? It's Charlie.'

'Charlie's the murderer? I don't believe it.' But then for an instant I thought of Margot saying that because he was the most unlikely murderer he was the most likely.

'No, no, no,' Felix said. 'But he told us who the murderer is. I was fairly sure of it myself, but he completely cleared it up. Now first thing tomorrow we're going to Brighton. Or I'm going. You needn't come if you don't want to.'

He sprang to his feet and went out of the room.

Brighton!

I had never been there and knew no one there. I could not think of any reason for going to Brighton, unless it was for the sea air, and for that there were nearer places along the coast.

Not for the first time in my life I wondered if Felix had taken leave of his senses.

Over our supper we were almost silent. I knew the mood that Felix was in and that to try to make him talk would be useless. He was completely absorbed in something that was going on his mind, but it might not be anything important. Important, that is to say, to me. His sudden desire to go to Brighton might be merely because he had suddenly remembered that he had some commitment there which was going to interfere with his concentration on the murder in Allingford. But if he was sufficiently mysterious about it I might go on believing, so he might be thinking, that I would not resent his leaving with his job here undone. On the other hand, perhaps he really believed that there was something to be found out in Brighton that had some genuine connection with the death of Kate Galvin.

For the moment, however, I knew that the more I pressed him, the more mysterious he would become. The omelettes that he had made were very good, but he gobbled his up at great speed, declined the biscuits and cheese that I offered him, then went out to the hall and started telephoning. I could not hear what he said, but when he came back to the kitchen where he had eaten he looked a little more relaxed.

Sitting down at the table once more and after all helping himself to a biscuit and some of my Cambozola, he said, 'I should think we could get to Brighton in two hours, don't you?'

I got up and started to stack the dishwasher.

'So I'm going with you, am I?' I said.

'I told you, that's just as you like.'

'I'd prefer to know why I'm going.'

'Oh, didn't I say that? I'm sorry. But I told you I'd been to see Dr Cairns, didn't I?'

'Yes, but he doesn't practise in Brighton.'

'No, of course not, but he gave me Dr Raven's address and telephone number. I've just been talking to him and made an appointment to see him at eleven o'clock tomorrow.'

'Dr Raven? But he's been retired for years,' I said. 'He was Mrs Lovelock's doctor once, but Dr Cairns has been here for quite a long time now.'

'Yes, and this man Raven settled in Brighton when he retired,' Felix said, 'and he may be able to tell us something of the greatest importance. Perhaps not. I don't suppose he took his medical records with him and his memory may be failing by now. He's pretty old, I imagine, isn't he? So we may have our trip for nothing. But it's worth trying.'

'All because of something Charlie told you?'

'That's right.'

'I don't recollect that he told us anything of importance, unless it's something to do with that key he found, or the one in the garage that may or may not have been locked.'

'I've said, forget the keys, haven't I? No, this is something much more extraordinary and I'd really sooner not talk about it till I've thought out all its implications. Something that worries me is that Charlie could be in danger. That's why I don't want to waste time, but mean to get moving tomorrow.'

'You say that Charlie knows who the murderer is. Is that why he's in danger?'

'Of course. He doesn't know he knows, but still if he did let it out to the wrong person anything might happen. Well, are you coming with me?'

'Oh yes, I don't want to be left out of things, even if I don't know what they are.'

'Good, I'm glad you'll come because it'll be useful to have someone there who can be a witness to whatever Dr Raven tells me.'

'You wouldn't feel like giving me just a teeny-weeny hint about why you want to see him?'

'All right. Nick Duffield's ears.'

'Aren't they perfectly ordinary ears?'

'I thought so myself, but Charlie doesn't.'

'I wonder if ears, like keys, are symbolic of anything,' I said. 'I've heard it said that large earlobes are supposed to indicate a sensual temperament. Have you any views about that?'

'None at all. It doesn't sound very convincing to me. Anyway, we'll have to have breakfast fairly early and get going not later than nine o'clock, or say half past eight to be on the safe side.'

I switched on the dishwasher and as the humming sound

of it filled the kitchen and I was reaching for the sink-basket where Felix had left the shells of the eggs that he had used for the omelettes an astonishing thought came into my mind.

'Charlie doesn't think . . .' I began, then stopped. All of a sudden I did not want to talk about the matter any more than Felix did. If what had occurred to me was not complete nonsense, then it needed very careful consideration. I took the eggshells out to the dustbin, then said that if we had to have an early breakfast next day I was going to bed now. Felix said that he would like a bath and asked if he could have the bathroom. I left it to him, went to my bedroom, but then instead of going to bed, I sat down in a chair there for I did not know how long, trying to sort out my tangled thoughts.

At last I went to bed and spent a restless night, sleeping and waking and sleeping briefly again, troubled by senseless dreams that chased each other in confusion through my semi-consciousness. So at last it was a relief to get up and go downstairs to make coffee for breakfast.

The morning was another of the beautiful kind that can happen in October. The sky was a pale, clear blue, the sunshine was bright but cool, the trees along our route to Brighton were changing to a deep, rich copper. For most of the way we drove along motorways and the traffic in the earlier part of the morning was heavy with commuters making their way to London. But before we reached the end of our journey it had eased off and we were early for our appointment with Dr Raven, so we parked our car near to the sea-front and spent a little time strolling along it. The sea was calm and glittering and there were not many people on the beach. A child playing with a dog put me in mind of poor Boz, but I did not want to talk about him. I did not want to talk about any of the new thoughts that were occupying my mind, any more than Felix evidently did about what were in his. I felt that if I was too far wrong he would only mock me, yet there was something more to the matter than that. There was a kind of fear of what it might lead me into, which amounted to fear of my own thoughts. We talked about Felix's new work and about theatres he had been to and about a holiday in the High-lands that I had taken only a few weeks before, and then, punctually at eleven o'clock, presented ourselves at the home of Dr Raven.

It was in a flat in a terrace of converted bow-fronted Regency houses, not far from the sea. Mrs Raven let us in. I remembered her from her husband's days in Allingford, though she had aged a good deal since I had seen her last. She was a short, plump woman with white hair which in the old days had been almost black, dark eyes that had not lost their brightness, a small, heavily wrinkled face and a bent back. She led us into a cheerful-looking sitting-room which had a curved bay-window that faced the street and a probably recently installed Adam-style fireplace in which an imitation log fire was alight, its gas-fuelled flames leap-ing up with monotonous steadiness above the synthetic logs. She told us to sit down and that she would bring her hus-band and some coffee.

He came in a moment later, shook me heartily by the hand and said that it was very nice to see me again. He was a tall old man who I thought was a little over eighty, with wide shoulders that stooped only a little, an almost bald head, but with bushy eyebrows above bright brown eyes and a square brown face with a tan which, no doubt, was the result of the fact that he might still go swimming in the nearby sea. He was wearing a loose sweater, tweed trousers and slippers.

I introduced Felix to him, told him how well he and Mrs Raven were looking, said that I hoped the move to Brighton had been a success, then left it to Felix to explain the purpose of our visit.

Dr Raven introduced it himself, however. 'I suppose what's brought you to see me is something to do with the tragedy in poor old Mrs Lovelock's house. Very sad. Very upsetting for poor Miss Cox. How is she, by the way?'

'Considering everything,' I answered cautiously, 'she could be worse. It's in the newspapers, is it?'

'Oh yes, and it was on television in the News of the South East,' he said. 'Didn't you see it?'

'No, but I haven't been watching it much for the last day or two,' I said.

'And of course young Cairns rang up and told me all about it,' he went on. 'And he said he rather thought I might have a visit from you two. Now what can I do for you? It's a number of years now, as you know, since I last saw Helen Lovelock.'

'What we'd like to ask you, Dr Raven,' Felix said, 'is if you remember an occasion when her grand-nephew, Nick Duffield, was attacked by one of the bull terriers that she used to breed. I think he would have been eleven or twelve at the time.'

'Goodness me, yes,' Dr Raven said. 'Poor little chap. I had a great argument with Helen about it. I told her the dog, once having tasted blood, was dangerous and ought to be put down. But she wouldn't have it. He was a valuable beast for breeding purposes, apparently.'

'Can you tell us what damage he did to the boy?' Felix said. 'Was it serious?'

'Well, it was distinctly unpleasant. He tore a bit off one of the boy's ears. Bit him in neck too, but that healed satisfactorily. There was nothing much to be done about his ear, though. That's to say, it healed all right, but it left a scar. Not that that matters so much nowadays when men can wear their hair down to their shoulders if they're so

inclined, covering up their ears. I seem to remember that
the boy grew his hair a bit long right away, because I
suppose he felt self-conscious about the ear. Not that the
damage was serious, but I suppose he thought it was more
conspicuous than it was. And it's a very frightening thing,
I should think, to be attacked by a dog. One's so accustomed to thinking of him as man's best friend. Then suddenly seeing those bared teeth, the wild eyes, the gaping
jaws, hearing the snarling . . . Oh dear me, I shouldn't be
talking like that, but after that episode I was always a bit
frightened myself of Helen's dogs. I'm a cat man myself.
We have three cats.'

'The most frightening animal I've ever seen,' Felix
remarked, 'was a crocodile. I'd seen pictures of crocodiles,
of course, and always thought they were sinister-looking
creatures, but it wasn't till I was once in Uganda in a boat
on the Nile and the beasts were lying gaping in the mud at
the edge of the river, that I saw for the first time that the
inside of those terrible jaws is bright yellow. I don't know
why bright yellow should have seemed a peculiarly terrifying colour. After all, in some circumstances, red can be a
very frightening colour too. It's the colour of blood. And
we aren't too surprised if the inside of some animal's jaws
are almost black. But the bright yellow was a shock. There
was something unnatural about it.'

'So you've been up the Nile, have you?' Dr Raven said
with interest. 'I've never been in Africa myself. Yellow,
now. Is that really so?'

'Yellow as a canary,' Felix said.

'Funny thing, but I never knew that. You've travelled a
good deal, have you?'

'Well . . .' Felix began, but I interrupted warningly.
'Felix!'

'Hm, well, a bit,' Felix said. 'But we mustn't take up too
much of your time. I wonder if you also remember another

boy who'd have been a bit older than Nick Duffield at the time. His name was Charles Bordman.'

Mrs Raven came into the room just then with a tray of coffee and a following of three cats. They came to investigate me, then Felix.

'Charlie Bordman,' she said as she put the tray down and started to pour out the coffee. 'Oh yes, I remember him. A dear child, though not quite normal. Retarded, is that the word? He seemed to get stuck mentally at about ten years old. Such a tragedy for his mother. She was a very gay, attractive young woman in those days, but she gave up everything to look after the boy. I believe her husband left her eventually because he couldn't stand the situation. Dreadful, really. But why were you asking about Charlie?'

'I was just wondering if you know if he might have been there when the dog attacked Nick,' Felix said, 'or if at least he might have remembered the event.'

'I really don't know,' Dr Raven said. 'I don't think he was there. Perhaps he was, but if so, I can't recall it. It happened in Mrs Lovelock's garden. They summoned me very urgently, because they wanted me to give the child an injection against rabies. Unnecessary in the circumstances, because the dog was a perfectly healthy beast, only as savage as that breed sometimes can be. And there was nothing I could do about the torn ear, except put in a few stitches. But it could all have been a lot worse.'

'But do you think that Charlie, who's now getting on for forty and still with a mental age of ten or thereabouts, could have remembered that all this time?' Felix asked.

'Quite possibly,' Dr Raven said. 'After all, it's the same with all of us. Here am I, eighty-two, with a memory that's sadly impaired, but I could tell you in detail a lot about the friends and ememies I had when I was ten, how I met them, what we did together, why we liked each other or why we fought bloody battles. But ask me the name of that nice man with whom I had such an interesting conversation last week and what we talked about, and my mind's a complete blank. If Charles Bordman ever knew what had happened to Nick Duffield when they were children, I think he might have a quite clear memory of it. But why do you want to know?'

Felix looked evasive. He stooped to stroke one of the cats.

'It's just that it's arisen in a rather strange way in the murder inquiry,' he said. 'Charlie made an odd statement yesterday that we wanted to check. My wife is an old friend of Anna Cox and Miss Cox is very anxious about Nick Duffield, whom the police seem to suspect. Quite wrongly, I feel sure. But the incident of the dog may be of some importance.'

We escaped soon after that and made our way back to the car.

While Felix was negotiating our way through the traffic of Brighton I did not try to talk to him, but once we were doing a steady seventy on the motorway I said, 'Why did you say the police are wrong, suspecting Nick? Or this man who calls himself Nick Duffield. Because he's an impostor, isn't that what you think?'

'That's clear enough, I should say,' he replied.

'And was it only when Charlie said his ears were odd that you thought of it, or had your brilliant mind already deduced it?'

'My brilliant mind was fairly sure he was an impostor as soon as I heard the whole story from you. But it was Charlie's statement that confirmed it. To him it wasn't natural that Duffield should have two normal ears. The drama of losing a bit of one must have made a deep impression.'

'But what made you think of it first?'

'Simply that if a strange young man turns up from Australia after twenty years just to make friends with a rich old woman who's certain to die fairly soon, it's natural to make sure that he really is who he says he is. It wouldn't surprise me at all if the police have already started checking on that.'

'But he knew so much about his childhood,' I said. 'He seemed to know a lot about Kate and the dogs, and he knew about having been attacked by one of them. And he told me about how his parents died.'

'Oh yes, he must have known the real Nick Duffield very well. They must have spent a good deal of time together somewhere.'

'And what do you suppose happened to the real one?'

'My guess is he's dead, or he'd have come over himself to claim his inheritance. Of course one of the things that made me suspicious of our Duffield here was what you told me about his throwing those letters into the fire. There had to be a reason for it, and one could be that it suddenly struck him that there they were in the handwriting of Mrs Lovelock's real nephew, and though it might have been easy enough for this chap to learn to forge a mere signature, it would be a different thing to forge all the writing that was in what may have been quite long letters.'

'Then do you think he murdered Nick Duffield to be able to step into his shoes?'

'I haven't the least idea. That's strictly a matter for the police, here or in Sydney.'

'But considering the cold-blooded way he murdered Kate, mightn't it be that murder is a habit of his?'

The sign of a service station had appeared beside the road.

Felix said, 'I think we might pull in here for some lunch, don't you?'

'But he did murder Kate, didn't he?' I said. 'Like Charlie, she saw that the bit of his ear that ought to have been missing was there and realized that he couldn't be

Nick. Only she wasn't quite sure of it at once and took a day or two deciding whether or not she could be mistaken. I remember when I saw her that evening before she was killed she seemed in a rather uncertain state of mind about him. I thought she was only uncertain about whether or not she liked him, but I think it may have been uncertainty about his being the real Nick she remembered. Then she decided he couldn't be and she threatened him with exposure, and so he shot her. He made up his mind to seem to set off for London, and gave poison to Boz so that his barking shouldn't wake Kate or Anna when he returned, shot Kate and then set off for London again to set up an alibi for himself. Only the fog scared him and he didn't go after all.'

'Do you think the man we're talking about would have been scared by a bit of fog?'

'But it must have happened like that, mustn't it?'

Felix swung the car off the motorway and into the car park of the service station.

I had a very good reason for hoping that he would agree with me, but he answered, 'You're wrong. You're absolutely wrong.'

CHAPTER 10

We went into the cafeteria and bought fish and chips and cups of tea. I like fish and chips, but when we sat down at one of the tables I felt so repelled by the thought of eating that I pushed mine away from me. Sipping some tea, I stared for a moment at Felix, who had started to eat with the signs of a good appetite.

'So it was Anna,' I said.

'I'm sorry,' he said. 'Truly sorry, Virginia. I know you're fond of her.'

'I've always admired her,' I said. 'She seemed such a brave old woman. She seemed to be making the best of growing old.'

'So she was in her way. She was certainly enterprising.'

'When did you begin to suspect her?'

Strangely enough, now that we could talk of my own suspicions, which had been a dark cloud in my mind since the evening before, I felt better.

'Oh, from the first,' Felix said. 'I thought there was something strange about her wanting me to come to Allingford. I mean, what could I do about the murder that the police couldn't do much better than me? You know as well as I do that I'm no genius. If she acted as if she thought I was, it had to be pretence, didn't it? So what was her motive?'

'Well, what was it?'

'To help her to get Nick Duffield, or whatever his name is, out of trouble. To pick up all the clues about him that would clear him. It was very important to her that he shouldn't be so scared by what had happened to him that he'd take off for Australia before he'd inherited his fortune and she'd really got her hooks into him. If he began to feel that his charade was too dangerous, he wasn't going to stay around much longer, and once he'd gone he'd be out of her power. Incidentally, I wouldn't be surprised if we don't see him again. Instead of going to London to see Bairnsfather, my guess is he went to Heathrow. I dare say he's out of the country by now.'

'I suppose she knew from the start that he wasn't the real Nick Duffield.'

'I should think so. She'd have seen at once that there wasn't a bit missing from his ear as there ought to have been. I don't know when she tackled him about it. Not too soon, I imagine. I should think before she took any steps she wanted him to be accepted by everyone as the Nick Duffield he claimed to be, as well as having him get used to the feeling that Mrs Lovelock's money was within his grasp.'

'But why didn't Mrs Lovelock notice that there was anything wrong about his ear?'

Felix went on eating his fish and chips and after a little more hesitation I took a tentative mouthful of mine.

'Her eyesight,' Felix said. 'It may not have been as good at eighty-eight as she thought it was. And he was kind to her and affectionate and he seemed to know everything about the family that was to be expected, and she wanted him to be Nick. Of course he was no use to Anna until he'd certainly inherited Mrs Lovelock's money.'

'Then you mean . . .' Again the fish and chips nearly choked me.

'They'll never prove anything,' Felix said. 'Helen Lovelock is dust and ashes. But I wouldn't be surprised if her quiet death was caused by having a cushion pressed carefully over her face. Think of Anna's position. She'd been working for the old woman for something like thirty years, and she knew that her reward at the end of it was going to be a miserable five thousand a year. I expect she tried hard to persuade Mrs Lovelock to make a new will, more in tune with present day prices, but if she did, she didn't succeed. But there was the young Australian, ripe to be blackmailed once he had his share of Mrs Lovelock's wealth. I may be wrong. Perhaps Anna had the heart to let Mrs Lovelock live her full span of days. But I can't help thinking of that cushion.'

'Then everything was upset by Kate coming home.'

'That was the first thing that went wrong,' Felix agreed. 'I don't suppose Anna dreamt she'd come over for the funeral. She let her know of her aunt's death as a matter of course to keep everything looking as normal as possible, but she didn't think Kate and Nick would ever meet. And once she'd got what she wanted out of him and he was safely back in Australia, she was quite happy to let him enjoy the rest of Mrs Lovelock's wealth. And after all, what she wanted from him wasn't so very greedy.'

'Just her expenses in a good old people's home.'

'That seems to have been all.'

'And you think that when he'd fixed that up with the lawyer she'd have left him in peace.'

'I think she was shrewd enough to do that.'

'But Kate came home and she didn't notice his ear at first, but then she did and got uneasy and after a day or two discussed it with Anna and may have started saying that they ought to have some proof of his identity, is that how it happened? And Anna decided she'd got to be killed. But where did she get the gun?'

'I expect Mrs Lovelock had it stowed away somewhere. We've only Anna's word for it that she hadn't. Old Lovelock, who was in the First World War, may have brought it home with him. And Anna worked out a very careful plot. She decided she'd do the murder on an evening when Nick Duffield, to go on calling him that to save trouble, would be on his way to London with a cast-iron alibi. That was very important. It was going to spoil everything for her if he was suspected. Then she invited a collection of Mrs Lovelock's friends to come to the house and choose mementoes of her. And one of the things about that whole situation that struck me straight away as strange was that all those friends of Mrs Lovelock's should have had such good reasons to hate Kate Galvin. That was a bit unusual, wasn't it?'

'I didn't hate Kate,' I said, 'but I was invited.'

'Who invited you? Was it Anna?'

'No, it was Nick.'

'There you are then. I think you'll find the others were chosen by Anna. Nick, of course, had no idea of what she was up to, though didn't she tell you that evening that he was going to pay for her in that dream home of hers?'

'Yes, and said how good and generous of him it was.'

'So she must have tackled him by then and let him know what he was in for.'

'I don't think Paul had any reason to hate Kate.'

'But at least he might have wanted to get hold of the emeralds. He was a somewhat suspicious character and Anna wanted as many as possible of that kind around. And any of them might just have been able to poison Boz, though that was always a bit doubtful. The only people who'd certainly have been able to do it were Duffield, herself and Kate. But it had to be done to help build up the picture that the murderer had come in from outside and knew his barking had to be prevented. And it was just possible that one of the visitors in the house that evening could have had the whole thing worked out before coming and brought some poison along. Then everything was spoiled by the fog.'

'Didn't you say the fog wasn't important?'

'I think I said that if I'd just committed a murder and perhaps stolen some emeralds too which I thought were valuable, I shouldn't have stayed around, dumping the things in the garden. I'd have made off as fast as I could, fog or no fog.'

'And I said that meant you didn't think Nick was guilty.'

'And I don't think he is—of murder.'

'But why did the fog matter?'

'Because it made Duffield turn back. It wasn't really urgent for him to get to London that evening. If he set off early next morning it would be just as good from his point of view. And he didn't know the road and may even have got lost and thought that the obvious thing for him to do was to find his way home again. And he got home just after Anna had shot Kate and smashed the kitchen window. But she hadn't yet got away with the gun and the emeralds, as I imagine she was intending. If he hadn't come back just then she'd have driven off in her car, not worrying about the fog as she knew every inch of the neighbourhood, and dumped them in some pond or stream, and then gone quietly to bed, ready to find the body in the morning. But before she'd had time to leave she heard Duffield drive into the garage and realized that if she drove her car out he'd hear her too. So she put the necklace and the gun in the only place she could think of just then and I should think hoped that Paul Kimber would be suspected as she didn't know at the time that the emeralds were false and that he knew it. But then the one thing she'd guarded against happened. Duffield had no alibi and it was he who was suspected. Hence her invitation to me to come down and help to clear him.'

'I suppose it's important for a blackmailer to look after the welfare of the victim.'

'Of course it is.'

'And the doping of Anna's milk and the search of the house, I suppose Anna did that herself to make it look as

if there was someone murderous around who couldn't be
Nick as he was safely in police custody.'

'Oh yes, that's why I said all along the key wasn't important. I was sure it was an inside job.'

'And what are you going to do about it?'

Felix paid some more attention to what was left of his
fish and chips, then said, 'I don't really know.'

'You've no proof of it,' I said.

'That's the trouble.'

'Are you going to tell Dawnay about it?'

He sighed. 'I suppose so. Then I'll find he's got it all
thought out himself and he'll let me know he doesn't like
interference from amateurs.'

'All the same, you'll have to go.'

'All right, I will. And then this evening . . .'

'Yes?'

'I thought we might have dinner at the Rose and Crown.'

That was very nearly the end of the whole matter for me,
at least so far as solving the murder of Kate Galvin went.
The pain of it was going to take much longer to fade. Felix
drove me home, then drove on to the police station and I
did not see him again for about two hours. He never told
me exactly what happened during that time, but when he
returned he had a certain self-satisfied air which meant,
I thought, that what he had had to tell Detective-
Superintendent Dawnay had at least been taken seriously.
It was only later that I heard from my household help, who
I think I have said was the wife of a constable, that the
man whom I had known as Nick Duffield had in fact been
arrested at Heathrow, because by the time that he tried to
board a plane for home our police, as suspicious as ever
that he might be the murderer, had been in communication
with the Sydney police and had learnt that Mrs Lovelock's
real grand-nephew had been killed in a car crash there

when he was driving the getaway car in an armed raid on a jeweller's.

When that happened he had only recently come out of prison after serving a sentence of five years for robbery with violence and where, for a good deal of the time, he had shared a cell with a man called Mark Arnold, who had also been in on the raid that had ended in Nick Duffield's death, but had escaped from the wrecked car and disappeared. Still later I read an account in my newspaper of the trial of Anna Cox for the murder of Kate Galvin. The chief witness against her had been Mark Arnold. He had told everything about her attempt to blackmail him, admitted his attempt to impersonate Nicholas Duffield, from whom, in prison, he had learnt a great deal about Nick's early life, and was deported to Australia, where he was wanted for other crimes. Anna Cox's sentence was life imprisonment, so after all an old people's home of sorts was found for her, though at the expense of the taxpayer and not of Mark Arnold.

The question of whether Helen Lovelock's death had been murder was never raised.

But that evening when Felix and I had returned from Brighton, we had dinner together at the Rose and Crown. We had steak, salad, ice-cream and coffee. I did not enjoy it very much. That was not because of the food, it was excellent. But a deep sadness had taken possession of me. I had been fond of old Mrs Lovelock and also of Anna, whom I had always completely trusted, admiring her for her hard-working, sturdy loyalty and the apparent fortitude with which she had accepted the fact that only that wretched little annuity was to be her reward. She had seemed to glow too with gratitude for Nick Duffield's generosity to her. I felt that I would never trust my own judgement of other people again.

To try to make myself think of something else, I said,

'Whatever made you tell that ridiculous story to Dr Raven about crocodiles' jaws being yellow?'

'They are yellow,' Felix said.

'I dare say they are, but you've never seen one.'

'How d'you know? You don't really know very much about how I spend my time.'

'I do know you could never have been on the Nile. You're scared stiff of aeroplanes, and don't tell me it's claustrophobia, which is quite a respectable sort of illness to have. It's just that you're plain frightened. You think the plane will have a bomb on board, or be hijacked, or will smash into a mountainside or plunge into the sea. In fact it's a much safer form of travel than driving on our roads. You could fly round the world in much greater safety than you can drive out of my garage into Ellsworthy Street.'

'A very good reason for not driving out into Ellsworthy Street,' Felix said. 'But if I were to suggest just keeping my car there for a little too long, I'd find it wasn't welcome.'

'We won't talk about that,' I said. 'But do you know what I think you ought to do? I think you really ought to make up your mind to go round the world. At first it might be a strain fighting off the panic, but long before you got home you'd have overcome that and you'd have seen all sorts of things that you'd find far more fascinating than the things you make up.'

'And where do I get the money for that?' he asked.

'I'll contribute to it.' I was almost sincere when I said that, though I was quite sure that my offer would be rejected.

But he looked thoughtful for a moment and I found myself driven to sudden frantic calculating about whether or not I really could spare enough to buy him at least his ticket, if not to pay for his hotels and incidental expenses.

Then he chuckled. 'It was a nice try, Virginia, but I think I'll stick to my cleaning-ladies.'

'I thought you said they were mostly cleaning-gentlemen,' I said.

'That's right. And the business pays, which is more than can be said of some of the things I've done. I mean to make a big thing of it.'

That must have been true, for he paid for our dinner with his credit card.